Sour Lemon

and

Sweet Tea

The Sour Lemon Series, Book 1

Julane Fisher

Relax. Read. Repeat.

Gisella Sweet,
You can make a difference!

Julane Fisher

SOUR LEMON AND SWEET TEA
(THE SOUR LEMON SERIES, BOOK 1)
Published by TouchPoint Press
www.touchpointpress.com

ISBN 13: 978-1946920393
ISBN 10: 1946920398

Editor: Kimberly Coghlan
Cover Design: Colbie Myles, colbiemyles.net

http://www.julanefisher.com/

First Edition

Dedicated to Adell, one of four sets of twins and fourteen siblings...

Chapter 1　🍋　The Ghost

MY TWIN SISTER sits on the front porch kicking her legs back and forth off the edge. She fiddles with the long braid hanging down her back as we wait for our friends. I rest my elbows on my knees and stare at the blue sky, watching the white puffy clouds form into various shapes. One looks like a baseball diamond and a bird flies so close to it, it seems like he's dodging the ball as it soars out of the park.

The air is thick with humidity and sweat beads gather on my forehead in thick droplets. Sitting up, I swipe the back of my hand across my forehead. It's almost too hot to play baseball, but it won't stop me because I've been waiting for this day all year long.

"Good gravy, Ellie." Mama shakes her finger in front of Ellie's face. "Take off those Daisy Dukes and put on some proper clothing for a baseball game."

Mama points to Ellie's short-shorts, named for the character on my favorite television show, *The Dukes of Hazard*, a new show that comes on every Thursday night. The Duke brothers drive a car they call The General Lee, stirring up more trouble than Georgia dirt, and every girl in town wants to look like their beautiful cousin, Daisy.

Ellie's shorts are really just a pair of blue jeans that Mama picked up at a yard sale. Ellie took scissors and chopped them shorter than a pixie haircut.

As Ellie stomps into the house, muttering under her breath, I snicker because Ellie never gets in trouble. I'm the one always stuck in a tangled mess.

My family lives on a chicken farm in Triple Gap, a sleepy town forty miles north of Atlanta, where I know just about everyone, and where just about everyone I know is a farmer. We're the only farm in town with a baseball diamond built right in the middle of the front yard.

Since we live near Atlanta, my older brother Jesse wanted to name our team the Braves. However, since most of my brothers and sisters are twins, my brother Jimmy decided to name our family team 'The Twins'—as in the Minnesota Twins. It struck me as kind of odd because we don't live anywhere near the state of Minnesota. In fact, I didn't even know where Minnesota was until Jimmy showed me on a map.

Even though my last name is Liles, most folks call us the Twin Family and for good reason. Twins Jimmy and Jesse turned thirteen right before school let out. Ellie and I are eleven, but we turn twelve in July. My brother Billy is nine, and he happens to be the only Liles child born without a twin. Six-year-old twins, George and Grace make three sets of twins. Mama has always called George and Grace, 'The

Twins.' I have no idea why since nearly all of us are twins. Besides, it sounds like a baseball team.

Anyway, having more than one set of twins in any family is peculiar, but having three, like we do, is apparently uncanny—at least according to Mrs. Buzby.

Mrs. Buzby is our organist at First Baptist Triple Gap. For reasons I cannot begin to understand, she feels the need to endlessly mention to Mama that the multiple sets of twins in our family is weird. Well, she doesn't say *weird* because it's not polite, but that's what she really means. Mrs. Buzby ends every one of her sentences with "bless your heart," which gets on my nerves—as if my heart needs any blessings from her.

A truck the color of cherry tomatoes tears down our driveway stirring up red dirt and the tinted windows shield me from seeing who is inside. I'm pretty sure it doesn't belong to any of my friends because I don't know anyone that can afford such an expensive truck. When the door opens, a tall man with dark hair and piercing blue eyes steps out. He wears a black, three-piece suit with a tie that matches his eyes.

He stares at me, so I stare back, neither one of us speaking. It reminds me of the old Wild West movies I've seen on TV with the dust flying in the air and a man standing with his hands on his hips. I can almost hear music playing in the background as we yank our guns from their holsters. When a girl steps around the hood of the Ford, I'm jolted back into the present.

It's Violet—my arch nemesis.

Last year, Violet moved to town and was placed in Mrs. Periwinkle's class with Ellie and me. Mrs. Periwinkle was the nicest teacher I'd ever had. Violet, on the other hand, is the meanest girl I've ever known. She also happens to be the richest girl in town, so no one dares challenge her. Except me.

I have a habit of saying stuff right back to her whenever she decides to open her big, nasty mouth. Like the time she made fun of my favorite teacher. You have to laugh at the irony of a girl named Violet making fun of her teacher named Periwinkle. Although talking back has gotten me in more tangled messes than I can count, my words come flying out like a hawk chasing a rat.

Ellie strolls back out to the porch wearing shorts down to her knees and a red and blue striped shirt. "Can't believe Mama made me change clothes," she grumbles. Spotting Violet standing in front of me, Ellie stops.

Violet scowls at me sitting on the porch steps. "Why are you farm girls sitting around? Shouldn't you be working or something?"

"We're waiting for our friends to get here," Ellie smiles. "Everyone's coming to our farm today to play baseball."

"And you weren't invited," I growl, putting my hands on my hips.

Violet's eyes scrunch together, and she puts her hands on her hips too. "Who says I wanted to be?"

"Well you're here, aren't you?" Crossing my arms across my chest, I glare at her.

"I came with my daddy. He has business here." Violet nods toward the back of my house where her daddy disappeared. "He bought a brand-new 1979 Ford truck." She flips her hair over her shoulder and throws her nose in the air.

"So?" I say.

"So, it's the best there is. The fanciest model they make."

I roll my eyes and groan.

Violet scans the yard, her nose still pointed to the sky, when she spots my brother. Her ugly frown turns upside down. "Oh, hi, Jesse." Violet fiddles with her curls and bats her eyelashes.

I think I'm going to be sick.

"Uh, hi." Jesse frowns and turns away.

"What are you doing?" she asks.

"Um, practicing for the big game today." Jesse tosses the baseball in the air then catches it with his glove. "You here to play ball? You're awfully dressed up."

She looks ridiculous. Her pale pink dress has tiny blue flowers sprinkled all over, and a white bow rests below her chin. Her knee socks, pulled up high on her legs, are topped with white sandals. Considering I'm wearing jean shorts and a yellow and blue striped T-shirt, she is way overdressed.

Plus, it's ninety-five degrees out here. Violet's got to be sweating like a sinner in church.

"I don't play baseball. That's a boy's sport." She gawks at me.

Shuffling my feet in the dirt, I kick dust onto Violet's white sandals.

"What did you do that for? You're going to pay for that, smelly farm girl," Violet squawks like a chicken.

"Violet," Ellie interrupts. "Why don't I show you our tire swing while you wait for your daddy?"

Our swing is the one Pappy, my grandfather, built for Ellie and me. He took a tractor tire and hung it from a large branch on the old oak tree that nestles against the house. *Why would Ellie want to take Violet to our special place?* Moping, I stomp all the way to the swing.

Shouts echoing from inside the house lure me in as my habit of spying on the grownups kicks into high gear. Ellie says it's like stirring up a bee's nest and one day it's going to get me in trouble.

When Ellie catches me wandering toward our house, she wags her finger in front of her face. "One day you're gonna get stung, Lillie. I'm tellin' ya."

But I haven't been stung yet.

Slinking to the open back door, I press against the kitchen wall and peer around the corner. The back door slams shut making me cringe. Daddy and the man from the truck stand in the family room. The man waves a stack of papers in Daddy's face as Mama appears from the long hallway that leads to her room.

Spotting Mama, the man's scowl curves into a smirk. "Ruth. Good to see you again." His voice is as sweet as maple syrup. "You look as beautiful as ever on this fine afternoon."

Does Mama know this man?

"Why you no good, dirty..." Daddy starts to say something else, but Mama interrupts.

"What are you doing here, Duke?" Her voice is anything but sweet.

"We need to talk. I tried explaining all this to Tommy Ray, though you know him. He won't listen."

"Now is not a good time. We have a lot of children coming here today, so we are quite busy. I have to kindly ask you to leave."

"Hang on, now. Listen a minute. I've got a buyer for your land. It's a good offer."

"I told you, Duke. I ain't selling." Daddy's jaw tightens, and a vein in the middle of his forehead pops out.

"I think when you see this offer, you're going to change your mind." Duke continues. "Development is coming to Triple Gap, Tommy Ray. You can't stop it forever."

He must be talking about the shopping mall. Many folks think it's high time for the town to grow, since it is 1979 and all. It sounds exciting to me, but since almost everyone in Triple Gap is a farmer, they're not too keen on giving up their land to build shopping centers.

Daddy takes a step closer and points his finger in Duke's face. "Now you listen here. I'd rather lose my land than sell to the likes of you."

Lose our land? Am I moving? Where am I going to live? My heart beats in my chest making air escape from my lungs in heavy puffs.

"I'd be careful what you wish for if I were you." Duke scowls.

"Get off my property, you thief." The vein on Daddy's forehead pops out again.

"That's enough. Both of you," Mama shouts. "Tommy Ray, we'll need to finish this conversation another time." She glances over her shoulder and nods toward me.

Gulp. I've been caught. I duck behind the wall, but not before Daddy catches my eye. His face turns as red as a raspberry.

Oh no, I'm in trouble now.

"You need to leave, Duke." Mama's voice is like ice.

Keeping my body flat against the wall, I tilt my head back around the corner.

"Alright. But look this offer over, will you?" He hands her the stack of papers and walks down the steps. He reaches the bottom stair and turns back around. "This buyer already bought the piece beside you, so this may be your last chance."

Daddy opens his mouth to say something as Mama squeezes his shoulder. "Let it be, Tommy Ray."

My feet reach the back door when Daddy hollers. "Lillie Mae. Not a word of this, ya hear me?"

"Yes, sir."

Mama's face stiffens and her lips purse together. "My goodness, Tommy Ray," she whispers. "After all this time. I never thought...he's been gone for fifteen years."

As I stumble out the door, my legs feel like they've turned to stone. Violet sits on the tire swing, and Ellie dangles from a large nearby branch.

"You okay?" Ellie asks. "You're so...pale...like you've seen a ghost."

"Maybe I did." My body shudders. "Maybe I just did."

Chapter 2 🍩 Baseball

BASEBALL HAS always been an important part of my life. When Daddy built the baseball diamond in my front yard, it caused quite a disagreement with Pappy, who thought the land should be used for farming. But Daddy wouldn't hear it. He insisted his kids would grow up playing baseball.

My grandmother, Meemaw, says that when Daddy was young, he dreamed of playing baseball for the Atlanta Braves. Seems like he was famous at Triple Gap High School from all the pictures and newspaper articles, although something must have happened. For reasons no one will say, Daddy never did get to play professionally.

He says things like, "I want better for my kids," or "I don't want you kids to be like I was back then." When anyone asks what he means, he always responds, "It was a long time ago." That's it. End of discussion. Maybe that's why he decided to teach us to play.

"What happened to you?" my brother Jimmy yaps, stepping onto the pitcher's mound.

"Nothin'." I shrug my shoulders. "I was playin' in the dirt."

"Why?"

"Never mind," I say, rolling my eyes.

"Well hurry up and wipe your hands 'cause you're about to see the fastest pitch in the West." Jimmy throws his arm in the air in giant circles.

"We live in the South, Jimmy, for your information," I shout from first base.

He rolls his eyes "No duh, Lillie Mae. It's just an expression."

Jimmy stands on the pitcher's mound and shouts orders back and forth with his friend, Freddie Johnson, who is up to bat. Jesse crouches behind home plate, giving finger signals to Jimmy about where to throw the ball. He looks so official, though the truth is, Jesse spends more time praying that we will all get along than he does catching the ball.

Praying in my family is as natural as breathing. It's what we do when something isn't right. Most folks in Triple Gap go to church on Sundays and say their blessing at supper. But the way I see it, sometimes that isn't enough. No one understands this more than my brother Jesse. It's like he was born to be a preacher. He says the most beautiful prayers with lots of big, fancy church words.

When The Twins were born, they were really sick, so Jesse prayed for them every day. Mostly, he prayed that George would be alright so he could play third base on our family baseball team. Jesse figured we had him and Jimmy to play pitcher and catcher, and Billy and me for first and second base, so we needed a third baseman.

I thought it was a wonderful prayer.

"Waiting on a baseball to come to you is like waiting on God to answer your prayers," Jesse likes to say. "Sometimes it comes fast down the middle, but other times it's like a curveball you didn't see coming."

He's probably saying some prayer like that right now from behind home plate.

"Hey," Billy calls from second base. "Are we gonna play ball or talk all day?"

"Play ball," Jimmy announces like a true umpire. He throws a fast pitch, high and right.

"Strike one," Jesse hollers.

Jimmy grins. "That's what I'm talkin' about."

While we wait for Freddie to make a hit, Ellie and I talk about our birthday. Mama says turning twelve is special because we will be teenagers before we know it. She says this is our last year before *That Event*. I'm not sure what she means by *That Event*, but since Mama thinks it's special, Ellie and I plan to take full advantage of her excitement.

Pretty soon, we are arguing because Ellie thinks we should invite our teacher, Mrs. Periwinkle, to our birthday. "Our teacher isn't gonna come to a kid's birthday party," I insist.

"Well, I wanna invite her anyway."

"Well, I don't. The whole idea is stupid."

"It's not stupid," Ellie grumbles.

Freddie hits a pop fly above first base. I'm so distracted by Ellie's ridiculousness, the ball flies past me. Trying my best to snatch it out of the air, I land face down in the red, Georgia clay.

"Lillie Mae, stop talkin' and play the game," Jimmy barks.

"I am playin.' Ellie's talkin' to me is all."

Jimmy dashes to home plate. He's going to get mad at me, but I don't care. Baseball is supposed to be fun. Jimmy's been asked to play on an All-Star's traveling team this year, and ever since he got picked to play on that fancy team, he thinks he's the boss of all of us. While I brush the dirt off my shorts, Tift Johnson steals third base and dashes to home plate.

"Safe," Jesse shouts.

"Darnit, Lillie Mae," Jimmy hollers. "You let Freddie get a double. Quit squawking."

"Sor-rie." As soon as he turns around, I stick out my tongue. Ellie laughs.

"Beat ya again, Lillie Mae," Tift taunts from home plate. Tift and Freddie are brothers, and Tift always picks on me. "If you'd ever quit blabbing so much, you might actually be good."

"I can play baseball just fine, thank you very much," I shout back at Tift.

"Don't look like it," he snaps.

"Well, why don't I come over there and show you how I can throw the ball right into your face."

"Lil, knock it off," Jesse yells. That's what Jesse always calls me. Not Lillie, or Lillie Mae, just Lil. "Get back to first base and cool off. Tift, go on now, let it go."

"I thought we were here to play baseball, not watch a wrestling match," Freddie grumbles from third base. "I just made the best play of my life and all y'all can do is argue."

"He's right," Jimmy says. "Let's play some ball." Jimmy hops back onto the pitcher's mound and throws a curve ball right across home plate.

"Strike one," Jesse calls.

Jimmy cheers. "Now we're talking."

I'm not having a good game at all today. I keep thinking about the man who was here earlier. Daddy warned me not to say a word, but it's hard because Ellie and I tell each other everything.

A large bead of sweat trickles down my forehead and lands in my eye. *Ouch.* Taking off the glove, I rub my eye, smudging red dirt onto the side of my cheek.

Wade Green is up to bat and hits a low grounder along third. George tries to chase it down as Billy beats him to it. Billy scoops the ball and throws it to me. I miss.

"Come on, Lillie Mae. What's wrong with you?" Billy yells.

"There's nothin' wrong with me, thank you very much," I holler back.

"Well, why can't you catch? Maybe you should try being more like Ellie." Billy knows exactly how to make me mad.

I am covered head to toe in dirt and most of my hair attaches to my face rather than the braids. Knowing my face is caked in red dust, my eyes dart Ellie's way. She stands on the front porch in a freshly pressed outfit without a speck of dirt on her, and her hair hangs in a perfect braid down the center of her back.

"Sour Lemon, Sour Lemon," Billy chants at me.

From the time I can remember, Mama sat on the front porch watching us play baseball with a glass of sweet iced tea with lemon. According to Mama, a true glass of southern sweet iced tea has a sour lemon inside it, creating a symphony of opposite tastes on the tongue.

Ellie is as sweet as the iced tea we drink. There's so much sugar and goodness in her, she doesn't have a sour bone in her body. But I am like a sour lemon. Although you can have great tea without the lemon, the effect on the tongue is sure different.

Ellie started calling me a sour lemon because of my annoying habit of talking back. "You need to sweeten up, Sour Lemon," she'd say.

"I'd rather be a lemon than icky brown stuff," I'd retort. It was a stupid reply that made both of us laugh. Ellie and I never could stay angry at each other for very long. But being mad at Billy is another story.

"Oh, Sour Lemon," he chants. "Catch the ball."

"You better not call me that again Billy, or I'll pin you to the ground so fast your face will be eatin' dirt." Storming toward him, Jesse stops me.

"Stop it you two," Jesse intervenes. "Lil, what's gotten into you today?"

"He started it."

"Did not."

"Did too."

"Y'all quit acting like babies and play ball," Jimmy hollers from the pitcher's mound.

We're only halfway through the game, and it feels like a volcano about to erupt. Tift hits a high one right up the middle, caught by Shortstop.

"You're out of there. Three outs," Jesse says like a true baseball umpire. "Nice catch Shortstop."

Shortstop's real name is Charles Coleman the Third, named after his dad and his grandpa, but we've always called him Shortstop. He lives on the farm next to ours and was sick when he was a baby. Since Jesse's prayers for The Twins were answered, he figured he should pray for the Coleman baby, too. Jesse prayed for that baby to be okay because our baseball team was growing and soon we were going to need a shortstop.

Yep, that's right, Jesse prayed for Shortstop. That's what we called that baby from that day on.

Chapter 3 🍋 Spying

BY THE END of the week, I've played baseball every single day. *This is what summer is all about.* My brothers and I plop down on the front porch rocking chairs to escape the heat. Gulping a giant glass of sweet tea, I feel like my stomach is going for a swim in a pond. Ellie squeezes fresh cut lemon wedges between her fingers.

"Hey, Sour Lemon. You want one?" She points to the bowl next to the tea pitcher.

"No," I growl, folding my arms across my chest.

"Well, I thought since you've had an attitude lately..."

"At least I'm not Sweet Tea like you."

"Maybe you should try being sweet some time. You might like it." She raises her eyebrows up and down making her nose crinkle.

Maybe I'm jealous of Ellie because she's the pretty one between us. All the girls at school tell her so. Her brown hair curls perfectly on humid summer days, and her long, thin legs seem to go on forever.

Unfortunately for me, my frizzy hair is downright unmanageable most days, and I'm built like my brothers, with broad shoulders and short, stubby legs. Wearing one of Ellie's fancy dresses makes me look like I've got a tablecloth pinned to me.

Pappy's booming voice makes me whip my head around and my ponytail slaps me in the face. The front door is ajar, so I peer inside. Pappy sits on our yellow and blue flowered couch, and Mama's slumped over in a nearby chair staring at a stack of papers. Possibly the same ones Duke Holt gave her the other day.

My brothers run off to throw the ball, so I sneak around to the side of the house and spot an open window. After what happened with Mr. Holt and my parents earlier this week, I'm as curious as a yard cat.

Ignoring my brother's protests to come play with them, I whisper to Ellie from the window, "You gotta hear this. Come here."

"Lillie Mae, you better not go snoopin.' You know Mama doesn't like it."

"I wanna hear what Pappy's sayin' is all."

"Why? It's not your business."

"Shh," I say, putting my finger up to my mouth. "Keep your voice down."

I want to tell her, *because there's a stranger in town trying to buy our farm, and Mama and Daddy are upset.*

"Can he do this William?" Mama asks Pappy, her voice tense.

"He can, and he did."

"It's not right."

"No, it ain't. But you need to know in case he comes around here again. Don't you talk to him without me or Tommy Ray, ya hear?"

When Mama doesn't respond, I peer in the window, wondering if the *he* they are discussing is Duke.

Uh, oh. Pappy is heading straight for me.

I glide onto the porch steps like I'm sliding into home plate. By the time Pappy strolls outside, Ellie carries on a conversation with me like it's the most natural thing in the world.

"Hey, girls." Pappy grins. "How's the game goin'?"

"Good," I answer, twirling my braids in my fingers.

"Lillie Mae missed a pop fly, and Billy made a double. Jimmy's been yellin' at her ever since," Ellie chimes in.

So much for keeping secrets. Ellie let it all out. Wonder if she'll tell I was spying too while she's at it.

"Don't let those boys get you down, Lillie Mae. You're good just the way ya are. You remember that now, ya hear?"

"Yes, sir."

He takes a few steps then turns back around. "Oh, and Lillie Mae. You'd tell me if you'd heard somethin' you shouldn't have, wouldn't ya?"

Gulp. I've been caught spying. Again.

After supper, while my brothers play outside, I get sent to my room for what Mama calls *eavesdropping*. Ellie comes in a few minutes later and sits on the bed with me. My head hangs low, feeling sorry for myself.

"Hey, Sour Lemon."

"Hey."

"Sorry you can't come outside. Even if you did deserve it." She smiles. "You gotta quit spyin' on the grownups, Lillie. I want us to have a fun summer, and it isn't fun watching you get in trouble all the time."

"I know."

"Let Jimmy be the one in trouble instead of you." She giggles, and I give her a half-hearted smile.

Clearing my throat, I proceed to tell Ellie everything that has happened this week—about Duke and Daddy, the papers Mama was holding, and about losing our land.

"You shouldn't have listened to all that, ya know." Ellie stares me in the eye.

I'm not ready yet to agree with her. "What if we have to move? Where are we gonna live? I don't want to leave our baseball field and have it all dug up." My chest tightens, and a tear forms in the corner of my eye.

"You worry too much, Lillie Mae. None of that's gonna happen."

"What if it does?"

"Leave that to the grownups. It's their business." She may be right, but I still don't want to admit it. "Promise me you won't stir up the bee's nest anymore?" Ellie waits for an answer. "Lillie?"

"Okay."

"No. Pinkie promise me, Lillie."

We interlock our pinkie fingers, the way we've done since we were little, and recite our favorite saying.

Pinkie promise, sisters true. Twins forever, through and through.

Chapter 4   D House

FROM SUNUP to sundown, there's always work to be done on a farm. Like all the other growers in town, we have farmhands to make sure the ventilation systems are working properly and to keep the chickens fed.

What the farmhands do *not* have to do is clean the chicken houses. That's because it's my job. Every day, I stir the litter on the floor of each house. Then every other week, I put in new straw.

I hate the work. The smell makes my nostrils burn, and my insides turn flips. Even though my nose is covered with a mask, the smell trickles its way in. You'd think I'd be used to the smell by now, seeing how I live on a farm and all. But I don't think I'll ever get used to it.

On top of the stench, our nasty chickens can be downright aggressive. Guess they don't like when their space is invaded. My poor legs have been pecked more times than I can count.

Our four chicken houses sit on the east side of our property near the cornfields. Each one is identified by a letter, although I have no idea why they were named that way. There's A house, B house...well, you get the picture.

Today, Jesse and I stir the litter in D house when a nasty hen decides to charge at me. "Jesse!" I shriek. "Get her to stop. She's hurting me."

"Stop running and hit her with your fork."

Pointing the giant pitchfork at the hen, it acts like a shield. The chicken clucks at me.

I'm fixin' to kill this chicken. If she pecks me one more time, I swear I'll...

"That's it. See, Lil, she's backin' off now. You gotta show her who's boss."

"Easy for you to say. She don't bother you."

Jesse laughs. "Maybe she chases you 'cause you run. She doesn't have anyone to chase if you don't run."

"Whatever. I hate this house. I'm gonna call it a four-letter word that starts with a D."

"Don't you go sayin' that word out loud, Lil. Daddy will tan your hide for cursing."

"I heard Daddy say it."

"Don't mean you supposed to. Cursin' is against the rules."

"You sound like Ellie. You and Ellie, always followin' the rules."

"Well, maybe you ought to try it sometime."

There's no use in arguing with Jesse and no point in finishing my chore if he's going to tell Mama about me cursing.

"I'm leaving." I stomp out of that nasty D house as fast as my stumpy legs will carry me.

Ellie and Jimmy are finishing up in B house, so I don't bother staying. Instead, I march to the baseball diamond where Billy and George pull weeds. "Y'all wanna go exploring when your chores are done?"

George shoots his head in the air. "Yes."

"Sure, yeah. Okay," Billy answers.

Other than baseball, exploring in the woods is one of my favorite things to do in the summer. "Okay. I'll go tell the others."

A few days ago, my brothers built a fort back behind the chicken houses. They piled sticks to create walls, and Ellie and I placed pine branches on top for the roof.

We pretend we're shipwrecked on a deserted island and the shelter we built protects us from the storms. Our imagination goes wild as we create our little world.

"It's been twenty-one days on this island," Jesse says, "and we haven't found one good piece of food. If we don't get food by tonight, I think we may all starve to death."

"Wait," Billy whispers. "I think I see something over there. Jimmy, is that...a wild boar?"

"Shh," Jimmy replies. "Be very still." Jimmy slowly lifts his bow and arrow. Drawing back the string, he aims and shoots. The arrow goes flying through the woods, straight into the boar's chest. "Got it."

George starts squealing like a trapped pig. "Eeeee, eeee..." Ellie and I splash through the mud, causing the red clay to fly onto my bare legs.

"I think that's gonna cook up mighty fine," I say.

"Billy," Jesse shouts. "Help us carry this heavy guy over to the fire, and let's thank the good Lord we are saved."

We sit down on logs, our muddy feet in front of us, and pretend to eat our delicious supper of roasted wild boar.

Guess we forgot all about our real supper until Grace appears through the trees. "All y'all are late for supper. Y'all didn't even get supper ready. I did." Grace pats her chest with pride. "Me and Mama's already got it on the table."

Oh, no. Getting supper ready is my other chore.

Jumping up, I race ahead of the others and charge in the back door to the kitchen. Daddy nearly knocks me off my feet.

"What in the Sam Hill—" he hollers, pointing to the mud caked to my legs and the filthy path I've left across the entire kitchen floor. That's one of Daddy's favorite sayings, although who Sam Hill is remains a mystery.

"Sorry about the mud, Daddy. I'll clean it up."

Mama places creamed potatoes on each plate. I turn to the sink to scrub my hands with soap, talking a mile a minute. "Sorry I'm late, Mama," I say, huffing and puffing. "Me and Ellie lost track of time. We were playing in our fort when we decided we were starvin' to death and hadn't eaten in twenty-one days, so we went hunting and shot a boar and ate it for supper, and then we sat around thankin' the good Lord that we were saved." The story spills from my lips in one breath.

Mama doesn't respond.

Maybe I'm not in trouble after all. "Mama?"

"Lillie Mae, go on back outside a minute," Mama yells from somewhere down the hall.

"Grace said we were late for supper."

"You are. We'll deal with that later. Go on back outside now."

Stepping over my mud path, I hold my hand out to stop Grace and Ellie from coming inside. "We need to stay outside."

"But Mama told me to make all y'all come in," Grace argues.

"I know. Then she said to go back out."

"Why?" Ellie asks.

I shrug my shoulders. "I don't know. What am I, a mind reader?"

"I'm hungry," Grace whines.

"Come on Grace," Ellie answers. "I'll push you on the tire swing." A look passes between Ellie and me like she knows something is up. Sometimes we don't need words.

My brothers grab a ball and glove, oblivious as usual. Now is as good a time as any to find out if Jesse knows what's going on around here.

Strolling up behind him, I tap Jesse on the shoulder. "You know anythin' about Duke Holt? He was here at the house a few days ago."

Jesse tosses the ball to Billy. "Yeah. There's rumors flying around about him. Don't know what's true and what isn't." He catches the ball, then throws it back to Billy. "Moved here a few months ago. Supposedly has a buyer wantin' farmland in Triple Gap."

"Why farmland?"

"Not sure. I think he wants to build shopping centers. Rumor is he grew up in Triple Gap and left sometime after high school under *mysterious* circumstances." The way he says *mysterious* makes it sound like Duke is some kind of spy. "Made a name for himself in the banking industry, making his fortune from other's misfortunes." He shrugs. "At least that's what a boy at school told me. Anyway, last year he reappeared in Triple Gap bent on putting the local farmers out of business."

"That's weird. If he's from here, why does he hate the farmers?" I ask, puzzled.

"Don't know."

Something smells fishy. If I have to swim to the ocean floor to get to the bottom of this, I will do so.

"Hey, what are y'all talking about? You look so serious." Jimmy makes a funny face, then throws a ground ball to George who scoops it up and passes it to Billy. "Be right back guys."

I recite what happened earlier in the week, doing my best to remember all the details—so much for not breathing a word. "What I can't understand is why Duke is determined to steal *our* land."

"Did he say he was gonna *steal* it or *buy* it?" Jesse asks.

"Same difference from what I gather," Jimmy says. Jesse and I turn in surprise. Jimmy shuffles his feet in the dirt, but doesn't say anything else.

"Well?" I throw my hands in the air. "What have you heard?"

Jimmy glances around before answering. Then, he leans in close and whispers. "Heard he's forcing Shortstop's family off their land." He nods his head toward the woods. "Told them he had a buyer who would pay top dollar for their farm. At the last minute, the offer completely changed. They're stuck."

Suddenly it all made sense. Duke said someone bought the land next to ours. *Who is this mysterious buyer?*

"I expect that's why Daddy's fit to be tied now," Jimmy continues. "Comin' on our property tellin' us he's got a buyer. I wouldn't sell to him, or his buyer, even if it meant I was gonna lose my land." Jimmy's hands curve into fists, as his face starts to flush.

"Easy for us to say," Jesse points out. "But what if Daddy doesn't have a choice?"

"I don't want to move," I say, shivering.

"We need to pray for this Mr. Holt," Jesse says.

"I don't feel like prayin', Jesse. I'd rather punch his lights out," Jimmy retorts.

"Who is you gonna punch this time?" Grace bounds into me, nearly knocking me off my feet.

"No one. Don't worry 'bout it," Jimmy growls, marching off.

"Push me on the swing, Lillie. Please," Grace begs. "Ellie says she's too tired."

Glancing at Ellie, she shrugs her shoulders. "Alright, come on." I spin Grace around and around on the swing until my arms feel like they are falling off.

"Have you heard about Shortstop?" I whisper to Ellie.

"No. What about him?"

I tell her everything Jimmy said. "Of course, Jesse's solution is to pray. But he can count me out. If Duke is anything like Violet, he isn't worth praying for."

"I don't know, Lillie. Maybe Jesse's right. Maybe praying would do some good." I shoot her a look like she's crazy. "You know, sometimes I just wish folks could get along." She turns to face me. "Do you ever think about that, Lille Mae?"

She doesn't wait for me to answer. Good thing, because honestly, it has never crossed my mind.

"That's going be my birthday wish this year," she continues. "I'm going to blow out my candles and wish for everyone to get along."

There Ellie goes again. As sweet as a glass of southern iced tea.

Chapter 5   Family Meeting

A WEEK HAS passed since that peculiar night we were sent outside without a single explanation. Rumors are spreading like grass seeds, but no one knows the truth.

After eating a fried baloney sandwich for lunch, I burst outside, heading straight for my favorite tree. The smell of freshly cut grass from the tractor makes me smile. Hanging upside down off one of the biggest limbs of the oak tree, blood instantly rushes to my head. From this angle, watching Grace and Ellie doing cartwheels in the yard looks more like they are reaching for the stars. Below me, George pushes himself on the tire swing that hangs from a nearby branch.

"Can we please play now, Lillie?" George is relentless. He won't give up until he gets his way.

Grunting, I flip myself upright and jump out of the tree. "Okay, come on."

"Finally." He throws his hands in the air.

As my brothers take their positions on the field, Daddy strolls down the hill from the barn calling for Jimmy. "Ride with me to the hardware store, son."

"Um, yes, sir. I was gonna practice pitching today. My first tournament is only a few weeks away."

"Yeah, about that tournament. Well, come on now. I need you to help me load some things."

Jimmy takes off his glove. "Yes, sir." Carrying it in one hand, he saunters to the truck.

"I call pitcher," Billy shouts. Jimmy glares at him. "What? You aren't gonna be here, so I'm the best they got."

Jimmy shakes his head and climbs up into the cab of the Chevy. When the truck is out of sight, Billy pitches the ball to George.

"Strike one," Jesse shouts.

"Come on. You can do it, George," I say, patting him on the back.

"Strike two."

George practices his swing. "Wait for a good pitch," Jesse reminds him. He lets two fly past, then smacks the ball.

"There you go. Run," I shout.

Since we are only playing two on two, he easily makes it to first base. Now it's my turn. I swing and hit, landing a pop fly right near Billy.

He drops the ball, and I run with all my might past first and on to second, shouting to George. "Go home. Go home." George passes over home plate as I slide into third.

When Daddy gets home, Jimmy hurdles out of the truck and stomps to the house. By the look on his face, he's as a mad as a burglar who got caught stealing. Who knows what happened at the hardware store to make him so angry.

"Kids," Mama shouts from the front porch. "Come inside a minute, please. Your daddy needs a word with you."

"Mama, I is up to bat again," George complains.

Hands on her hips, Mama shakes her head. "I am up to bat," she corrects. "Come on. The game will have to wait."

"Aw." Kicking the dirt, George creates a cloud of dust around him before dropping his bat with a thud.

With eleven members in the Liles clan, including Meemaw and Pappy, family meetings are quite common. With Jimmy mad and the crazy things he told Jesse and me about the Coleman farm, something just doesn't feel right.

"I bet this is about Mr. Holt," I whisper in Ellie's ear.

"There you go again. Worrying too much." She shakes her head. "It's a normal family meetin' about our chores. Maybe you won't have to clean the chicken houses anymore."

"Now that would be worth celebrating," I cheer, raising my eyebrows up and down the way Ellie does.

When I enter the kitchen, Pappy and Meemaw are already seated, and the mood doesn't feel at all like a celebration. In fact, no one is smiling.

Spread out all over the kitchen table are pieces of mail. Daddy looks like he hasn't slept in a month. His wrinkled face is complete with black circles under his eyes. Mama's eyes are puffy like in the spring, when the yellow pollen decides to fall all over our yard. Maybe Jimmy's done something wrong again. He doesn't mean to be bad, but sometimes I think he can't help it.

"What are all the papers for, Daddy?" Billy asks.

"Bills," Daddy replies.

"What are bills?" Grace interrupts.

"Things we need to pay for," Ellie whispers.

"Cause of me?" asks Grace.

"Well, yeah. Some of them." Daddy rubs his eyes, making the black circles appear even darker. Then, he gets real quiet. Whatever he has to say must be very important. "Grace has been going to a new doctor to help make her well. She is gettin' a lot better, but it's expensive. With all the medicine and bills I gotta pay, well, I told Jimmy he can't play on the All-Stars team this year."

"It isn't fair." Jimmy drops his head onto his folded arms and starts to cry. I've never seen my tough, big brother cry.

"I agree," Daddy says, his face dropping. "And you know I'm sorry about it. I really wanted you to play. We just don't have the money."

"I'm sorry too, Jimmy." Tears fill Grace's eyes.

"Grace Ann, this is not your fault," Mama jumps in. "Don't you go apologizing when you didn't do anything wrong."

Jimmy wipes his cheek with the back of his hand. "It's okay, Grace."

I actually feel sorry for Jimmy.

"I thought she was gettin' better," Jesse stammers. "I pray for her every night."

"I know you do. We gotta pay her doctors, so you keep prayin', ya hear me, son?"

"Yes, Daddy." Jesse's voice trembles.

"Pappy and I let the farmhands go today, so we're gonna need everyone's help this summer."

Did I hear what I think I just heard? No one lives on a farm without farmhands! It's unheard of, and it's totally embarrassing. It's like announcing to the world, we're so poor we can't even afford to hire help. This is humiliating.

Daddy's still talking, but I'm not listening. My head swims in a pool of confusion. This summer is not turning out at all like I had planned. In fact, I think Daddy may have just ruined my life.

I don't know anything about raising chickens. I'm not even allowed inside the chicken houses unless I'm changing the litter. The thought of spending more time with those horrid hens has me breaking out in a cold sweat.

"It's temporary, until things turn around." Daddy stops and looks at each one of us. "There's more than enough of us to get the work done. Oh, and don't worry. You'll be back in school before you know it."

That's not what I want to hear either! What about my summer break? What about me playing uninterrupted baseball all day?

I've had enough. Without thinking, I blurt out, "Is this about Duke tryin' to steal our land?"

Ellie pokes me in the ribs and gives me the twin look.

"No one's stealin' anything from anyone, Lillie Mae," Daddy barks.

Mama gasps. "Where did you get that idea in your head?"

Jimmy's eyes go wide. I don't want to rat him out. "I mean—I just thought since he came by the house and all. Well, I don't wanna end up like Shortstop."

"Lillie Mae," Mama explodes.

"What's happenin' to the Colemans is very unfortunate," Daddy replies. "But that's not gonna happen here, so don't you go spreadin' rumors. Ya hear me?"

"Yes, sir," I whisper.

"Things are definitely different now that Duke Holt's in town. We're gonna need to work together to keep this farm up and running. Do y'all understand what I'm sayin'?"

"Can I still play baseball?" George's words leak out of his mouth. He must have read my mind because I was thinking the exact same thing. Covering my mouth with both hands, a giggle gushes out.

Meemaw taps my arm. "Enough, Lillie Mae."

"You can still play ball, George," Daddy answers, glaring at me, "in the evenings. You boys are gonna help me and Pappy build two new houses. Y'all need to get out there early 'fore the sun gets too hot. Keep your hats on so you don't burn."

Jimmy doesn't say a word, and I don't blame him. He worked hard all year to make that team.

"Lillie Mae. Ellie. Y'all ain't gonna clean the houses anymore."

"Well, thank the good Lord." *No more getting pecked in the legs.*

Daddy gives me a look of pure irritation. "The garden you helped plant last spring is blooming, so you need to pick the vegetables every day or they'll spoil. Corn will be comin' up in the fall. There's a lot to do between now and then."

Even though I'm not one bit happy about having to work all day, at least I'll be in the garden instead of the horrid hen houses. Since Daddy ruined my life, the least he can do is prevent me from having sores up and down my legs.

"What do I get to do, Daddy?" Grace pleads, wiping her tears.

"You're in charge of raising pullets."

"Pullets?"

"Yep, pullets. They ain't like our hens. Those are broilers. A pullet's only job is to lay eggs. So, we'll raise them till they're ready to start laying, then sell them to families that want fresh eggs. We're gonna get you some this weekend. Maybe the pullets will bring in the extra money we need."

Daddy winks at Ellie and me. Every farmer around here knows that selling egg-laying chickens isn't going to bring in much money. Daddy's trying to make Grace feel better, so for once, I keep my thoughts to myself.

"Okay, now that we understand we need to work together, you kids can go back outside and play. We'll start first thing in the morning."

Only no one moves. Things have gone from bad to worse.

Chapter 6 ❀ The Snake

IT'S EERILY quiet the next morning. The sound of spoons clanging on cereal bowls fills the room. No one does much talking. When Pappy's booming voice echoes in the kitchen, it startles me so much, I nearly wet my pants.

"Okay boys, let's get going. Grab your hats."

"Yes, sir," they answer, stumbling up from the table.

As my brothers saunter off to get hats, I stare at Grace eating her Cheerios. She doesn't look that sick to me. She's always had coughing fits, so I'm having a hard time understanding why she needs a special doctor, and why it costs so much money.

"Lillie Mae, did you hear me?" Mama asks.

"No, Mama."

"Stop day dreaming and go with your sisters to the garden."

"Yes, ma'am."

Ellie and Grace are already out the door. Following them up the hill, they sing a song we learned at church last week about flying away. It has something to do with heaven. Grace sings at the top of her lungs. She doesn't even sound sick.

I don't want Grace to be sick anymore, and Jimmy sure wants to play on that All-Stars team. Maybe I should think of a way to help them.

Strolling up the hill, I remember being excited about the garden. Pappy cleared the land on the edge of our woods where we like to make forts with his John Deere tractor. He spent days tilling up the soil.

The big day finally arrived when Mama handed Ellie, Grace, and me some seeds. Grace followed Mama around, planting carrots and turnip greens. Ellie planted yellow squash, and I planted pole beans. Mama said to drop one to two seeds in each hole. I liked the feel of the cool earth on my hands as I covered the seeds with soil.

That first week, I checked every day to see if anything had grown. Mama told me it would take more than a week to get a sprout, and standing over my seeds wouldn't make them grow any faster. But I watched them anyway. It felt like it took forever for anything to happen.

Then, one day, there it was. A beautiful sprout. Not just one, but what looked like hundreds, all peeking their way up through the dirt. They pointed toward the sun as if the warm air felt good on their stems.

Now that it's June, my beans are in full bloom, and I'm proud of my crop. Freeing up both hands for picking, I strap the bag Mama gave me across my chest and begin picking my beans. My bag fills up fast, so I take it off and set it in the dirt. Reaching down with both hands, something slithers in the dark soil. Screaming, I jump back so hard my bottom hits the ground.

"What happened Lillie," Ellie shouts, running toward me.

"A snake. It tried to bite me."

Ellie sees the snake and shrieks.

"What is all the hollering about?" Mama marches toward us, and Grace points to the soil.

"Lillie Mae saw a snake right there, and it tried to eat her," Grace says.

"Not eat me, Grace. Bite me," I correct.

"What color was it?" Mama asks.

"Black."

Mama exhales like her breath had been trapped inside her lungs forever. "Good. Black is good."

"It is?" I ask, unsure whether or not I believe her.

"Black snakes won't try to bite you. They run off the bad snakes. I'm sure you scared it is all."

It didn't look scared to me. All I know is I never want to see a snake in the garden again. Every time I reach down to grab a bean, I imagine black snakes slinking through the vines. Maybe helping Ellie will get my mind off the snake.

It doesn't take long before Ellie and I are doing more playing than picking. Ellie wiggles her body like a slithery serpent, sticking out her tongue. She looks so ridiculous, I burst out laughing.

Oh boy, here it comes.

When Ellie and I get in one of our twin giggling fits, it's all over. I laugh so much that tears well up in my eyes and spill onto my cheeks. When Ellie comes close to me, my giggles fly out of my mouth.

Ellie laughs so hard at me, she falls backward, knocking over her bucket of fresh vegetables, and I fall down on top of that spilled squash.

Mama and Grace stare at us lying flat on our backs in the black soil. Mama spots the bucket of squished squash and gasps. Now I can tell you, I've only heard my Mama *really* yell a few times in her entire life, and unfortunately for me, this is one of those times.

"Look what you've done!" she shrieks. "That's going to cost us at least five dollars."

We aren't laughing anymore. I take one look at that squash, and sure enough, it's as squished as a refried bean.

"Sorry, Mama." I hang my head.

"Sorry nothing, Lillie Mae. We have work to do, and you just earned yourself some extra. No baseball for the rest of the week."

"What? No." My eyes fill with tears, only this time it's not from laughing.

"Oh, yes. Plus, you and Ellie will be helping Meemaw in the kitchen every night this week after supper."

"Yes, ma'am." Ellie puts her head down and doesn't say another word.

But I'm mad. In fact, if Mama wants me to be sorry right now, she's out of luck.

"Ellie, pick up what's left of the squash, and put it back into your bucket. Lillie Mae, go back and attend to your beans."

Mama knows she has given me the worst punishment in the world. I mope back to where that black snake is waiting for me. And to think I can't play baseball all week. Everything is changing so fast.

My life, as I know it, is officially ruined.

After supper, my brothers get to go outside, while Ellie and I scrub dishes. We have an electric dishwasher that Mama uses every day, but she and Meemaw decide we need to be taught a lesson. They make us hand wash every last dish. Meemaw must have figured she'd cook some extra food because every pot and pan we own sits dirty in the sink.

Grumbling, I pour dish soap in the sink and watch as the bubbles rise up nice and fluffy. At least the liquid green soap smells good. Each pot gets washed, scrubbing food off. Ellie dries the dishes and stacks the pots and pans in the cupboard.

I don't want Mama to be mad at me ever again. The way I figure, if I do a good job with the dishes tonight, Mama will realize that her punishment was too harsh, and she'll change her mind and let me play ball before the week is up.

As soon as Ellie puts the last pot into the cupboard, Meemaw takes all the pans back out again and grins. "Since I got me two more dishwashers, I'm gonna cook us some bean soup."

I'm like a pot of soup about to boil over.

"Lillie Mae. Get the dried beans out of the bin and dump them into a pot of cold water," Meemaw says. "They need to soak all night so we can cook em' up tomorrow. Y'all need to get up extra early so you can cook the bean soup before headin' to the garden."

Ellie and I don't do much giggling after that. My fingers are shriveled, and my feet are throbbing.

Stomping to my room, I complain to Ellie, and this time, she's complaining too. Ellie scrunches her nose and waves her hands back and forth. "I don't wanna get up early to cook smelly beans."

Ellie, Grace, and I have always shared a room. Grace sleeps on a twin bed next to the bunk beds that Ellie and I share. My brothers are stacked in the room across the hall. Jimmy and Jesse in bunk beds, and Billy and George in twin beds next to them. Daddy says he doesn't know what he'll do when all his boys grow too tall for their beds, but for now, somehow they all fit.

One of the disadvantages of our small house is that all seven kids have to share one bathroom. I change into my flowered nightgown and wait my turn for the bathroom.

A few years ago, I asked my friend Mary Olivia Montgomery, who has her own bedroom, if she ever got lonely at night.

"No, why would I?" she answered.

"I don't know. I think I would."

I like having my sisters to talk to at night. Sometimes Ellie and I talk way too long and Mama has to come in and shush us. By the time I brush my teeth, Ellie and Grace are already in bed. Climbing up the ladder up to my bunk, I remember wanting to ask Grace about her doctor, so I climb back down. Grace is already fast asleep. Ellie's eyes are closed.

"Ellie," I whisper.

"Hum?" She opens one eye.

"What's really wrong with Grace?"

She rubs her eyes and yawns. "Mama says she has asthma. Dr. Hardy said she should've outgrown it by now. Only, she's hasn't."

"The breathin' treatments—are they for asthma?"

She shrugs. "I think."

"So," I pause before going on. "Why is she getting worse?"

"Not really sure. Somethin' about her lungs were bad when she was born. Remember when The Twins were little and Daddy came to tell us they weren't breathing right?"

"Yeah," thinking back to when they were born. I remember feeling scared that they were going to die.

"I think this new doctor is trying to figure out what else might be wrong. Guess her medicines are real expensive, too. Daddy seemed worried about being able to pay for them."

Hanging my head, I whisper. "I don't want anything to happen to Grace."

"Nothing's gonna happen, Lillie. We'll always be together."

Chills run up and down my spine.

MAMA WAKES Ellie and me before the sun can even think of rising. My room is pitch dark, and turning on the light may wake up Grace. Instead of getting dressed, I stumble my way down the narrow hallway to the kitchen in my flowered nightgown.

Mama pours the water out of the bean pot from the night before and spreads the beans on the white Formica countertop. Ellie sweeps the beans off the counter and into a new pot, shaking salt and pepper on top.

"Not too much," Mama cautions. "We'll cook them all day. By supper, they'll be nice and tender." She smacks her lips together.

Ellie and I lift the heavy pot from the sink and place it on the back burner of the stove so The Twins won't accidentally burn themselves. Washing the remaining dishes, I grumble under my breath. When Mama raises an eyebrow, I shut my mouth.

Mama takes buttermilk out of the refrigerator and pours it on top of the flour and shortening, forming it into a ball. The smell of fresh biscuit dough reminds my stomach that it's empty.

I sure hope Mama will let me eat a biscuit straight from the oven, with honey melting into the fresh dough. It feels like a little piece of heaven on my taste buds.

As I wash tomatoes and celery, Ellie peels carrots and onions. Reaching into the drawers, I take out two cutting boards and two knives sharp enough to chop off Jimmy's big toe.

"Chop them into small pieces, girls."

I'm so tired, I nearly chop my fingers off more than once. My eyes water from cutting onions, and the sour smell mixed with sweet biscuit dough makes my stomach churn. Chopping into small pieces is hard work and takes forever.

While I'm slaving away over a cutting board, my brothers devour hot biscuits lathered with butter and honey and drown their scrambled eggs with cold orange juice. My mouth waters. Chopping the last tomato, my fingers stick in place around the knife and I can't straighten them for a good minute. Once all my cut vegetables make it into the bean pot, I wash the remaining dishes in the good smelling green soap, and Ellie dries them and puts them away.

Since Mama's still mad at me, I don't dare ask for a biscuit. Instead, I do what any self-serving twin would do. I get Ellie to ask Daddy because he never says no to her. Like ever.

Ellie uses her sweetest, little girl voice. "Daddy." She even bats her long, thick eyelashes. "Can me and Lillie Mae have a biscuit now? We've cut up all the vegetables and placed them in the pot. We washed, dried, and put the dishes away."

Through a mouth full of scrambled eggs, Daddy mutters, "Ask your Mama if you've done enough." He doesn't even look up from his plate.

I can't believe my ears. Daddy telling Ellie no? Well, to be fair, he didn't exactly say *no*, but he didn't say yes either. This is too much. I can't take another second of this nonsense.

"Mama, please," I beg. "I'm so hungry, I think I'm gonna pass out." Giving her the most pitiful face, I squish my cheeks together like I've lost hundreds of pounds.

"Well, you need to think about that next time you decide to squish some squash."

Billy's head shoots up faster than a rocket ship. He snorts, making everyone else bust out laughing. I don't think it's one bit funny. Neither does Ellie. Her eyes fill with tears that pour onto her rosy cheeks, making my brothers laugh even harder.

"Cry baby, cry baby," Billy chants.

"Shut up, Billy," I yelp.

Daddy slaps the table with his fist. "That's enough, you two."

"Girls, you may have a biscuit now. But may this teach you a valuable lesson." Mama pauses as if she is expecting me to talk. "Well, what did you learn?"

"Never to squish squash?" I ask, just as serious as I can be.

Billy falls on the floor with laughter. Thank goodness Ellie is there to save the day.

"What Lillie Mae meant to say, Mama," Ellie says, glaring at me through her tears. "Is that we learned not to be silly while we work. We promise to be more careful next time."

"Thank you, Ellie," Daddy answers.

Mama frowns. "Yes, thank you, Ellie. Lillie Mae, fortunately for you, your twin sister seems to understand the importance of hard work. I hope you can learn from her."

Daddy places his plate in the sink. "Boys, run on out to the chicken houses and get the floors cleaned up. Pappy will meet you there this morning."

Mama takes Grace by the hand and leads her to the back door. "Girls, eat quickly and go get dressed. I'll take Grace on out to the garden."

"Yes, ma'am," I say, stuffing my big mouth with an entire biscuit.

I never want to squish squash again.

Chapter 8 🍋 The Mill

ONE SATURDAY a month, farmers from all over gather together at the Sawnee Feed and Supply, a place we call The Mill. It's one of the biggest corn mills in Georgia, and folks have been going there since the turn of the century.

Uncle Chicken's the owner. Honest to goodness that is his God-given name. Well, not the uncle part. In fact, no one knows for sure why he's referred to as Uncle. He's not my real uncle, and I don't think he's anyone else's either. He doesn't even have a family of his own. He was married once, but the whispers around town are that his wife took off years ago with a traveling vacuum cleaner salesman.

Uncle Chicken is old, and when I say old, I mean like the moldy piece of bread that came with Sue Saxon's tuna fish sandwich from the school cafeteria last year. She shrieked when she discovered the green, foreign substance. Tift Johnson thought it would be fun to pass the bread around the table. And it was funny. Until it landed in Jeffrey Trammell's homemade soup that his mama had packed for him. Jeffrey stared at it like it might come to life, and I felt downright nauseous. No one dared utter a word until Jeffrey asked to be excused. He never made it to the bathroom, if you know what I mean.

Anyway, when Daddy was a little boy, he remembers visiting The Mill and swears Uncle Chicken looked old then. Uncle Chicken's missing half of his teeth and rumor is they got knocked out in a fight with that traveling salesman.

But teeth or no teeth, Uncle Chicken has a mind like a steel trap. He can calculate numbers in his head up to the billions. I create crazy math problems just to see how long it takes him to formulate an answer and I already have a good one picked out.

Traffic is backed up today, perhaps because of the hot weather. On summer days, all the kids wade in the nearby creek. That water is sure going to feel good.

When we finally pull into the gravel parking lot, I leap out of our truck and head straight for Uncle Chicken. He's surrounded by a group of kids, but when he sees me, he stops what he's doing. The kids watch silently because they know what's coming.

"Well, if it ain't the old twin."

"I'm not old yet, Uncle Chicken."

His laugh is more of a silent chuckle. "So, whatcha got fur me today?" He winks. He knows I'm gonna try to stump him.

"Okay, ready? What is twenty-five thousand, three hundred and seventeen times forty-seven thousand, eight hundred and fifty?"

He pulls his lips over his gums, and moves his jaw around like he's thinking hard. Then he spits out the answer before I can even blink. "One billion, two hundred eleven million, four hundred eighteen thousand, four fifty."

The crowd whoops and hollers. *How does he do that in his head so fast?* I think everyone is more impressed that he can come up with an answer so quickly than whether it's right or not.

"Dang, Uncle Chicken. How do you do that?" My mouth hangs open and my eyes are as wide as flying saucers.

"School, Lillie Mae. Ya gotta stay in school."

Still shaking my head, I bound down the hill to look for Mary Olivia. We've been best friends since the third grade. Her sister, Sarah Montgomery, one year older than us, is Ellie's best friend.

Mary Olivia stands in the creek wearing a pair of red and blue plaid shorts and a red shirt. She looks like an American flag. Sneaking up behind her, I whisper in her ear, "Boo."

Mary Olivia jumps. "You scared me, Lillie Mae." She is so easy to scare. "The water feels good today." Stepping in the cool stream, she hugs me. "I miss seein' you, Lillie."

We haven't gotten together since the beginning of summer break. All I do is work, work, work. Sometimes I call her on the phone to get the latest news, but I'm not allowed to talk for more than five minutes at a time.

"Ties up the phone lines," Daddy likes to bark. I sure hope one day someone will invent a way for me to take another phone call at the same time I'm talking to Mary Olivia.

"Missed you too," I say. "Have you noticed the entire town of Triple Gap is here today?"

"Haven't you heard?" Mary Olivia's face lights up in surprise.

"Heard what?"

"About the bank."

"Bank?" I have no idea what she's talking about.

"About Duke Holt. He made himself the chairman at the bank."

My eyes widen. "You mean he bought the bank?"

"Shh." She pulls me in close, looking around to be sure no one listens. "Yeah, basically. Since most of the farmers have their loans there, it means Duke's now in charge."

"And I'm the last to know?" I had a bad feeling about that man the minute he stepped out of his fancy red truck.

"Your daddy called for an emergency Farmer's Association meeting." She places a strong emphasis on *emergency*.

Grabbing Mary Olivia by the arm, I drag her out of the water. "Come on, we gotta go listen."

She pulls her arm away and stares at me in total shock. "You mean spy?"

I shake my head knowing full well that this is not the first time Mary Olivia has spied on grownups. "Don't you ever do that at your house?"

"No, not really."

"Yeah, right." I roll my eyes. "Well, we do it to each other all the time. Actually, *I* do it all the time. That's what happens when you have so many in your family. I prefer to call it good detective work. Now, come on before we miss it."

The Twins splash in the water, so they won't notice I'm gone. Billy's got himself a good size trout on the line, and George helps him take it off. No doubt they'll be busy for a while. Mary Olivia and I sprint up the hill, squatting down on the side of building closest to the parking lot.

Peering around the corner to get a better look, there are at least thirty farmers gathered around. From the expression on their faces, it appears they are in the middle of a serious discussion.

"Something has got be done 'bout him." The man shouting owns the largest pig farm in the county. "I vote we move our loans first thing Monday morning. It's not the only bank around."

"If we all ban together, there won't be a thing Duke can do about it." Mr. Johnson spits on the ground.

Pappy nods toward Mr. Montgomery. "Well, heck, you know all too well about the loans. Tell the others."

"You're tellin' me," Mr. Montgomery hollers. Mary Olivia's eyes widen. "Went to the bank yesterday to ask for an extension. Somehow my interest rate is higher now than last month. Nearly lost my head arguing with Duke. He's got me all tied up. Don't see how I can get another loan when I can't pay the interest on this one."

"That's not right. Something has to be done," Mr. Johnson snarls. "Duke thinks the sun comes up just to hear him crow."

Everyone talks over each other, and I can't make out most of what they are saying.

"Tommy Ray," Mr. Montgomery interrupts the shouting. "Duke's been pushing you around long enough. If there was ever a time to stand up to him again, I think the time is now."

Something about what he says disturbs me. About standing up to Duke *again*? Did Daddy know Duke Holt before a few months ago?

"I'm not gonna end up like...well, y'all know who." Mr. Montgomery continues. "It's high time we put a stop to this."

Grumbles and complaints fill the air.

Daddy yells above the noise. "Alright, we all agree. We'll threaten to move our money if we don't get the loan extensions we deserve. And we'll look for lower interest rates at other banks."

"Agreed."

That's my cue to run before I get caught spying. Turning around, Mary Olivia and I crash into Jimmy. Freddie and Tift stand next to him.

Opening my mouth to scream, Jimmy smacks his hand over my mouth. Yanking his hand off my lips, I yelp. "You scared the willies out of me."

"What are y'all doing here?" he barks.

"Same thing you're doin'. Spying."

"Girls are so stupid," Tift growls. "Lillie, you couldn't be quiet if your life depended on it."

I don't know why Tift always picks on me. I've known him since I was born. Ellie says he has a crush on me, but the thought of Tift liking me makes me want to throw up.

"Shut up, Tift," I growl.

"Both of y'all shut up 'fore we get caught," Freddie whispers. "Let's get outta here. They're comin' this way."

Mary Olivia and I bolt down the hill and discover Ellie and Sarah haven't moved. Billy and George throw fishing line into the creek over and over.

"Well, what did they say?" Ellie eyes me. I give her a look like I don't know what she is talking about. "Of course I know you went snooping, Lillie Mae. You can't help yourself." She smiles.

Sarah's not paying any attention to us. That's because she's making ooey-gooey eyes at Freddie, although I doubt Freddie evens knows she exists.

"You wouldn't believe what we heard, Sarah," Mary Olivia babbles. "Our daddy was mad 'bout that loan stuff that happened to us. I think there's gonna be trouble at the bank this week."

"Um, hum," Sarah mumbles.

"Did you hear me?" Mary Olivia tries to get her sister's attention.

When Sarah doesn't answer, I butt in. "Hey, Freddie. Have you seen Sarah around today?"

Sarah whips her head around. She's looks like a homegrown tomato. "Stop it, Lillie."

Everyone bursts into laughter, except for Sarah, who buries her face in her hands. The funniest part of all is that Freddie ignores me. Boys are so clueless.

As we pull down our long driveway, Daddy backs the truck up to our red barn. Pappy stands in front of the barn door, arms folded across his chest.

"Hey, Pappy," I call out, carrying a bale of straw. He brushes past me without a word. Glancing over my shoulder, Pappy and Daddy shout at each other, and Daddy's arms fly in the air.

Without warning, Daddy hops back in the Chevy and drives off. The tires spin, making gravel fly in the air, nearly hitting me in the head. Ellie and I exchange a startled look.

"Where's Daddy goin'?" Jimmy asks Pappy.

"To the Coleman's farm."

"Why? What's going on?" Jesse burrows his eyebrows together.

"Nothin' to worry 'bout, Jesse. Y'all finish stacking everything in the barn, then go on home." Pappy carries a load to the barn.

By the time Jesse and I come out of the barn and secure the double doors shut, Mama tugs Grace and George down the hill toward home. "Y'all come on. Everyone into the house. Right now." Mama turns around to be sure we follow.

But my eyes are on Jimmy.

Along our stretch of the woods, a path leads to the Coleman's farm that Jesse created years ago to make it easier to visit Shortstop.

Jimmy heads right for that path. Glancing between Mama and Jimmy, I know in an instant what I'm going to do.

Chapter 9 　Short Stop

"YOU COMIN' with me or what?" I stare at Ellie. She hesitates, so I take off running.

"Ellie Jean. Lillie Mae. Get back here this instant," Mama hollers from the front porch. I don't turn around. The way I see it, as long as Jimmy and Jesse are in on this with me, we can all serve our punishment together.

"I don't know if this is a good idea," Ellie says, huffing and puffing.

Throwing my arms in the air, I bark, "Of course it is. Come on. And for Pete's sake, keep up this time."

Sprinting as fast as my legs will carry me, I hop the fence dividing our land from theirs and head to Shortstop's house.

"Lillie. What are you doin' here?" Jimmy whispers. He and Jesse crouch down near the crawl space on the side of the house.

"I could ask you the same thing."

Jimmy glances over his shoulder as Ellie makes her way toward us. "You brought *her* with you? Are you crazy?"

"No, I'm not crazy, Jimmy. She's my twin. She followed me."

"So help me, if we get caught 'cause of you and Ellie, I swear I'll—"

"Y'all hush," Jesse interrupts. "Ellie. Hurry up and get over here."

There we are, the four of us, watching wide-eyed as Duke Holt shouts at Mr. Coleman. Taking a pen out of his white, button-down shirt pocket, Duke hands it to Mr. Coleman. "Sign here," he barks, pointing to the piece of paper he's holding.

"I most certainly will not. You have no right. This is my land."

"We've been over this. The bank owns this land now. When you don't make your payments, there are consequences." Duke speaks in a slow, deliberate tone.

"I made my payments every blasted month till you came around."

"Yes, that's true. But you were always late. With the interest piling up, plus the late fees, well, now you're six months behind. I've done everything I can to help you—"

"You didn't do anything to help us." Mr. Coleman's face is red with anger, and he curses under his breath. "I asked the bank for an *extension* not an *eviction*."

"What's an eviction?" I whisper.

"Shh."

Without warning, Mr. Coleman suddenly lunges at Duke, nearly knocking him to the ground. The pen goes flying, and the piece of paper falls to the dirt. Daddy grabs Mr. Coleman's arms and pulls him back.

"Don't," Daddy snarls between clenched teeth. "He ain't worth it. Trust me, I know. We'll figure out another way."

In all the chaos, I failed to notice that Shortstop was clinging to Jesse, his face as white as a sheet.

Chapter 10 🍋 A Crush

OUR TELEPHONE buzzes this morning like bees to honey. Mama attempts to whisper into the receiver, although her whisper is loud enough for the furthest neighbor to hear.

"I know. I can hardly believe it. Poor Louise," Mama repeats to every caller.

Ignoring the screeching sound of the phone ringing, I get dressed for church. Last winter, Mama decided Ellie and I were old enough to dress more like ladies. She makes us wear pantyhose to church no matter what the temperature. According to Mama, a lady should never attend church without hosiery.

It's hotter than a pan of fried chicken in my house, and sweat drips down my legs. The flimsy fabric of the white pantyhose gets caught on my nail leaving a snag mark. Reaching in my closet, I pick out a pale, green dress and a pair of white sandals.

Ellie looks beautiful in her misty blue dress and matching shoes. A simple brown barrette holds her hair off her face, and curly ringlets fall near her ears. Yanking at my frizzy curls and gathering them into a bundle, I can't duplicate Ellie's perfect appearance.

I suppose the only good thing about wearing hosiery on Sundays is I get to sit in the front of the truck on the way to church with the air vent blowing on me. My brothers have to sit in the bed of the truck where it's hot.

When we pull into the parking lot, I march through the front door of First Baptist Triple Gap, not bothering to say hello to the ushers. My eyes barely have time to adjust from the bright sunlight to the dim church lighting before Mary Olivia grabs my arm and drags me to the back pew.

"I tried calling you thirty times. Kept getting a busy signal," she complains.

"Not surprised. Our phone hasn't stopped ringin'."

Mary Olivia pulls me in close. "Everyone's talkin' about what happened to Shortstop. You've gotta hear what people are *sharing.*" She puts her fingers in the air making quotation marks when she says sharing because everyone knows that gossiping in church is wrong.

Mary Olivia prides herself in knowing the latest news. For someone who pretends not to spy, she sure does know the comings and goings of folks around here.

Take, for instance, a few years back, when Jed Eaves left his wife for a lady from Pickens County, who he claimed made him happier than a pig in mud. I don't know what it was about that lady that made him want to live in the mud, but his wife went crazy. And of course, I heard all about it from Mary Olivia.

"Did you see Shortstop? Is he okay?" Her eyebrows crease together.

"Yeah, I saw him…" Pausing, I glance around and whisper, "What if that was us? Or y'all?"

Mary Olivia doesn't answer. Her eyes go wide, and I follow her gaze. *Mama.*

"Lillie Mae. Time to go to our seats." Mama's lips squeeze together, and she doesn't wait for me to finish my conversation. Giving me a gentle nudge, she leads me toward our pew.

Our pew is the same row that the Liles family has occupied since Daddy was a little boy. Every family at First Baptist church has an unassigned church pew. You pick one, and you stay there for the rest of your life. No one is allowed to sit in your seat, and you don't dare move to someone else's. What's really embarrassing is that we occupy not one, but two rows. We're the only family in town that takes up more than one pew. In fact, when Ellie and I were born, someone had to move out to make room for us.

Sliding into my unassigned seat, a boy glances my way. I've seen him at church once or twice, although I've never paid him much attention. I don't even know his name. He smiles. Assuming he's smiling at Ellie, I search for her.

Is he actually smiling at me?

The boy has sandy-blonde hair hanging on his forehead, and he's wearing a navy-blue suit. He looks over and catches my eye. I look away, embarrassed.

The blaring tones of organ pipes interrupt my thoughts. The choir takes their seats, and Pastor Eddie welcomes everyone from the pulpit. We sing a few songs from the hymnals, the organ trailing along. Then, Mrs. Buzby moves to the piano and leads us in "I'll Fly Away," Grace's favorite. I cover my ears as Mrs. Buzby sings at the top of her lungs, not one note in tune.

Pastor Eddie asks for prayer for our neighbors in need. Although he doesn't mention any names, I assume he's speaking of the Coleman family. Out of left field, he suddenly asks for prayer for Grace Liles. Feeling the weight of everyone's eyes on me, I slouch down in my seat. I hate when attention is drawn to our family. Mama jabs me in the ribs with her elbow, forcing me to sit up. By the time Pastor Eddie dismisses us, I shoot out like an arrow leaving its bow.

Rushing to the Sunday school room, I plop down in the row of chairs where Ellie and I always sit with Mary Olivia and Sarah. Glancing over my shoulder, Cute Boy sits a few rows back. That's what I'm going to call him since I don't know his real name. Not wanting him to catch my eye, I put my hand to my head and pretend to fiddle with my hair.

"Hello, boys and girls. My name is Emma Marsh. I'm your new Sunday school teacher."

Emma Marsh is young and pretty with long blonde hair and big brown eyes. I can tell instantly that Jesse likes her because he smiles at her every time she asks a question. Plus, his hand pops up before any of us have time to think about what she asked.

"Why yes, Jesse, that is correct," Miss Marsh says the entire hour. "Would anyone else like to answer?" No one does. We all know Jesse understands everything about the Bible, so there's no point in any of us even trying.

Near the end of the lesson, Tift decides to tease Jesse. "That's right Jesse. You're so smart," he mocks in his best impression of Miss Marsh. He pretends to flip long blonde hair off his shoulders, making my brothers snicker.

"What's so funny, boys?" she asks. Poor Miss Marsh. I sure hope someone prepared her for junior high boys.

"Nothin', Miss Marsh," Tift answers in a high, girly voice. The snickers grow louder.

She turns to the girls, and Ellie gives me the twin look, moving her fingers over her lips like a zipper to keep my big mouth shut. "I don't know what's so funny, Miss Marsh," Ellie butts in. "I like this lesson, and I'd like to hear more."

Leave it to Ellie to save the day.

When Miss Marsh dismisses us, Mary Olivia jumps out of her seat. "Gotta run. Fried baloney sandwich day. My favorite."

"Mine too. See ya." Whipping my head around, I look around for Cute Boy, but he's gone like a flash. Linking my arm through Ellie's, I drag her to the parking lot. "Did you see that Cute Boy lookin' at me?"

She raises her eyebrows. "What boy?"

"Sittin' a few rows behind us. Sandy-blond hair, brown eyes. He smiled at me, Ellie. *Me.* Can you imagine?"

She frowns. "Since when do *you* notice boys?"

"I guess since today," I say, giggling.

Ellie shakes her head. "Who are you and..." She moves her head side to side. "Where's Lillie?"

Chuckling, I smile ear to ear. "I don't know what's come over me."

"Me either." Ellie flips me around to face her. "Wait a cotton-pickin' minute. Does my twin sister have—"

"A crush?" A smile fills my face. "I think I do."

Ellie whistles. "Oh, boy. What will Mama say to this?"

Grabbing Ellie's arm, I start to sweat. "No, Ellie. Don't. You can't tell Mama."

An awful, mischievous grin comes over her face. "Why?" Seeing the look of horror on my face, she bursts into laughter, doing her funny up and down eyebrow thing. "I'm just messin' with ya."

"Not funny," I pout, crossing my arms across my chest.

"Oh, come on. Yes, it was. I never thought I'd see the day my twin sister had a crush on a boy."

We ride home in silence, not wanting Mama and Daddy to know about the boy. Besides, Ellie and I have all day to talk to each other. That's because we're grounded for running off and spying at Shortstop's house.

Daddy was madder than a cat in water and grounded Jimmy and Jesse too. Come to think of it, I don't think Jesse's ever been in trouble.

After eating a quick lunch, we are sent to our room for the rest of the day. I fall onto Ellie's bed, the familiar creaking of the mattress echoing in my ear.

"Now, tell me all about it," Ellie squeals. "Who is this boy makin' my sister smile?"

"I don't know," I grin. "He sure was cute."

"Yeah, you've said that. A few times." She rolls her eyes.

"Why didn't you talk to him?"

"No way. I wouldn't know what to say."

"Good point. You're not too good at this kind of thing."

"But you are." My eyes go wide. "You can talk to him for me."

"Oh, no. No way," she protests.

"Please?" I bat my eyelashes the way she does to Daddy when she wants her way. "You're good at this kind of thing. Boys are always lookin' at you."

"That's not true," Ellie argues.

"Yes, it is, and you know it. Boys think you're beautiful. But I'm, well, plain."

Ellie giggles. "You're beautiful in your own way, Lillie. Besides, you are my twin, so you can't be that ugly."

"Hey." I push her down onto the mattress causing it to squeak.

She smiles. "You know what I mean. You're pretty, too, so don't you ever go thinkin' otherwise." She pauses. "We need to find out who this boy is and you're gonna talk to him next week. All you have to remember is to smile and say hey."

But that one word, *hey*, makes me so nervous, my insides jiggle. The really hard part is I have to wait who knows how long before seeing him again.

Chapter 11 🍋 Ice Cream

THE SWELTERING heat hits me when I walk outside. My shirt is soaked, and my frizzy hair sticks to my face. As the hot sun continues to bear down, Mama promises we'll get a break soon. Staring at Grace lounging in the shade makes me wish for a second that I was the youngest.

"Hey, George," Grace says. "Whatcha doin' here?"

George collapses next to Grace.

Great. Even he gets to be in the shade.

"Meemaw made homemade ice cream for us," he pants.

"Ice cream?"

"Yeah. Daddy said we can take a break. Mama, can the girls come?"

"Can we? Please?" Grace begs.

"Oh, well. That's a nice surprise." Mama wipes her forehead, smudging dirt across her brow. "It is hot and that sounds fun. Sure. Go ahead."

"Come on." George grabs Grace by the hand and drags her to Meemaw's.

Setting my bag away from the garden, I'm careful not to squish anything. At least that's one lesson I've learned this summer. No more squished squash for me. Taking off my gloves, Ellie and I join hands and dash away before Mama changes her mind.

Meemaw stands on her back porch holding a huge container of vanilla ice cream.

"What's the special occasion?" I ask. There must be a reason we get ice cream in the middle of a workweek.

"Pappy said you kids have been workin' nonstop and thought y'all needed a reward, so I came up with this idea. Got me some cream from the Johnson's farm last time I was there and made it into ice cream for all y'all."

"Thank you, Meemaw," I say, wrapping my arms around her waist.

"You're sure welcome." Meemaw hugs me back.

Filling my bowl to the brim, I park myself on the steps next to Jesse. "Meemaw said y'all have been working hard on the houses." My mouth overflows with ice cream.

"Yep," he says through stuffed cheeks.

"Glad for it because I get to eat your reward." Smiling, ice cream squeezes out of my teeth.

Jesse shakes his head. "No thanks to you, Lil. You gotta stay out of trouble."

Stuffing more ice cream in my mouth, I shrug my shoulders. "It's just the way I'm made. I can't help it."

"Yes, you can. You can choose to do right anytime you want. Ask God to help you."

Based on what just happened to my friend Shortstop and his family, I'm not sure God wants to hear what I have to say right now.

Dismissing the thought, I change the subject. "I miss playing ball."

"I'm sure you do." He raises his eyebrows. "We didn't play much the week you got in trouble, ya know. Wasn't near as much fun 'cause Jimmy didn't have anybody to pick on." This makes me chuckle. "Jimmy's still real upset about not being on the All-Stars team."

"Maybe that's why he's so mean," I mutter under my breath.

Jesse ignores me and takes a bite of ice cream. "Did you know the processing plant's been talking 'bout not doin' business with family farms anymore?"

Taking my spoon out of my mouth, my eyes grow wide. "Can they do that?"

"Yeah. If the farmers don't make enough money, Silo Farms will move their broilers to bigger farms."

My ice cream melts in the bowl. Trying to scoop out what's left, the cream dribbles down my chin, and I wipe it with the back of my hand. "Is that gonna happen to us, Jesse?"

"Not sure. Daddy hopes once E house and F house are built, Silo will send more chickens to us." He stops and looks around before continuing. Then he whispers, "All our money's goin' toward payin' Grace's doctors. Daddy got behind on his payments and...well...Duke Holt isn't givin' any extensions. Not to Shortstop. Not to us. Not to anyone. Pay it or else."

Frowning, I set my bowl on the porch suddenly feeling chilly. "Or else what?" Not sure whether I wanted to know the answer.

"It means we may lose our farm, Lil."

My whole body shivers, leaving a trail of goosebumps up and down my arms.

My bones ache from working hard all week. The way I see it, if I work hard and stay out of trouble, maybe Daddy can keep the farm.

It's mid-June and the garden is in full bloom. My beanstalks rise so high, they remind me of the *Jack and the Beanstalk* storybook Mama read to me a thousand times when I was little.

Right alongside the beans are loads of zucchini, squash, tomatoes, cucumbers, lettuce, radishes, and carrots. It's amazing the amount of work it takes to grow vegetables. There are so many beans, it takes Ellie, Grace, and me all morning and most of the afternoon to get them picked.

After lunch, we load baskets of freshly picked vegetables to take to the farmer's market. As I load the last basket into the back of the Chevy truck, Mama pulls me aside. "I'm proud of you for working hard this week, Lillie Mae. We have a plentiful abundance."

"What's *penniful* mean?" I ask.

"Plentiful means we have a lot of food." Mama slams the tailgate shut and smiles. "Your beans are perfect."

Mama calling my beans *penniful* and perfect makes me swell with pride.

The farmer's market on Highway Nine sits right next to The Mill. Every Friday afternoon for the rest of the summer, we're going to sell our homegrown vegetables there. Mary Olivia's family shares the booth with us, which means we finally get to see each other every week.

Proudly displaying my beans on the table, I'm hoping to take a minute to go say hello to Uncle Chicken. I've got another math puzzle for him to solve, and I can't wait to see how fast he can spit out an answer. A shiny silver car pulls up to our stand and out steps a very tall lady in a silky suit. She must have come all the way from Atlanta because folks around here don't dress like that.

"I grew them beans all by myself," I tell her. "Them is the freshest you can get."

"*They* are the freshest, Lillie Mae," Mama whispers.

Mama wanted to be a teacher before she started having so many kids, so correcting our grammar is her way of teaching.

"Sorry," I say to the beautiful, tall lady. "I've been trying to work on my grammar this year, but it don't seem to stick. My teacher, Mrs. Periwinkle, said my grammar is atrocious."

Mama lets out a loud sigh. Guess I didn't use correct grammar again, only this time, Mama doesn't bother correcting me. Maybe because the pretty lady grins at me.

"Young lady. I'm proud of your hard work. You keep it up, and you're going have yourself one plentiful crop," she says.

There's that word again. "Thank you, ma'am." She must really like green beans because she bought every last one.

Mary Oliva watches her drive away. "What's that woman going to do with all those green beans?"

"I have no idea," I say, shaking my head. "I was wondering the same thing."

At the edge of the booth, Grace sells the baby chicks faster than crows can fly. "That there's Peck. And this one is Pick. She's my favorite. You can have both of them for the right price."

Daddy would be impressed with her sales ability. I think folks like that she took the time to name them because she sells every last one.

"Don't get too excited," Mama warns. "We have to take that money and buy more pullets."

"Why on earth would we do that?" Grace gives Mama a look like she's crazy.

Mama winks. "Because you are the best chicken seller I've ever seen."

Hum, maybe I will choose to do right after all. It does feel good. Well, kind of.

Chapter 12 Bullies & Bees

MONDAY MORNING, I'm still brooding from not seeing Cute Boy at church yesterday. My outfit was perfect. A blue dress, hosiery, and matching shoes. My hair was, well, let's just say it was manageable.

The pastor droned on and on about something, but I didn't hear a word. I was too busy looking for Cute Boy. He wasn't in church, and he wasn't in Sunday school. That got me thinking. His family may not be the church-going type. Mama will never approve of a boy that doesn't enter the church building every time the doors open.

The latest gossip from The Farmer's Association meeting has been unusually quiet, and that's got me all stirred up today too. Mary Olivia told me that she hasn't heard a thing about what happened at the bank with all those farmers. I've been trying so hard to be good lately that I haven't had time to spy.

When Mama announces we are going to Sawyer's Gifts and Market this afternoon, I'm as happy as a butterfly flit-floating on lavender. Sawyer's, located downtown on the square, is a few doors down from the bank.

It's a beautiful gift shop. On one side, stacked to the ceiling are collectibles and expensive gifts, and the other side is a grocery market. It's a small store compared to the Food Giant down the block, but Mama and the manager at

Sawyer's, Earl Rumsfeld, went to Triple Gap High School together, and Mr. Rumsfeld agreed to buy her vegetables.

Ellie and I work all morning, stopping only for lunch. By three o'clock, we head downtown, our baskets over-flowing. Grace stayed home with Meemaw, so Ellie and I get to ride in the cab of the Chevy.

Ellie reaches for the radio dial on the dashboard, and on comes Sister Sledge's hit song, "We Are Family." It's my favorite song. Reaching for the volume, I turn it all the way up. "This could be us one day, Ellie," I shout above the music.

"Not the way you sing." Ellie laughs, and Mama covers her ear closest to me.

"We are family. I got all my sisters with me. We are family. Get up everybody and sing."

With Ellie and me singing at the top of our lungs, everyone in town can probably hear us. When Mama pulls into a parking space in front of Sawnee Community Bank and turns off the engine, the radio goes silent. I sure want that radio to come back on.

"I need to stop by the bank before we go to Sawyer's," Mama says, unloading the baskets.

The bank? What a stroke of good luck. Maybe I can get some news about what is happening with the farmers and I won't have to spy.

Walking in the front door, the sunlight blinds my vision and I run smack into someone. Opening my mouth to apologize, I stare into the blue eyes of Duke Holt. Forgetting my manners, I give him a frigid stare, hoping he'll turn into a frozen statue. All I can think about is what he did to Shortstop's family. He smiles at Mama, but she doesn't smile back.

"Hello, Ruth. Good to see you again."

"I have a lot to do today," she snaps. "So, if you'll please excuse me." She tries to step around him as he blocks her path to the teller counter.

"Did you look over the offer I left with you?"

"No, Duke. We told you. We are not selling."

"It's a fair offer, Ruth. You might want to reconsider."

"We are not going to reconsider. Now if you will please excuse me."

"Is there a problem here?" A short, chubby man comes charging up next to Duke. Sweat beads form on his bald forehead.

"No, no, there's no problem." Duke smiles. "I was telling Mrs. Liles what a great piece of property she has."

"Well, I expect that Mrs. Liles knows she has good property. I imagine she's here to make her deposit and get on her way. Isn't that right Mrs. Liles?" It wasn't really a question. "Mr. Holt, perhaps you and Mrs. Liles can discuss that property at a later time."

"I expect we will," Duke replies. He moves toward what looks to be his office, then turns around and glares at Ellie and me. "Girls. Tell your daddy I'll be back up to your house soon."

My teeth clench together as anger fills me from my head to my toes. "My Daddy don't want you there, so don't come by again."

Mama's face registers utter shock. Ellie shudders. The short, bald man's mouth hangs open so wide, I expect a bird's nest could fit inside.

"I suggest you keep your thoughts to yourself," Duke growls, moving back toward me. His face flushes, and his fingers curve into fists.

"And I suggest you leave my family alone," I shoot back.

"Lillie Mae Liles. That is enough. Don't you say another word," Mama shrieks. Calling me by my full name is a clear indication that I'm in t-r-o-u-b-l-e.

"Please, Mrs. Liles," the bald man interrupts, as sweat drips onto his cheeks. "Y'all step into my office."

Mama grabs my hand and yanks me toward the office door. She squeezes me so hard, I'm sure all my bones are going to break.

She sits in a brown, leather chair across from the man's desk. Bending my legs, I start to sit in the second leather chair when Mama stops me.

"I've changed my mind. I think it's best you wait outside," she says. It isn't up for discussion.

Ellie's face drains of all its color. As soon as I step back outside in the sweltering heat, Ellie lets me have it. "What did you do that for, Lillie Mae? You got yourself in a heap of trouble, smartin' off that way to an adult."

"I don't know. I get so mad sometimes that the words come flyin' out."

"Mama is *so* mad at you."

"Yeah. I know." Shuffling my feet, I feel sort of bad. Then, I picture Shortstop watching helplessly as Duke steals his home. "Mr. Holt makes me madder than a wet hen."

Ellie ignores me and waits for me to calm down. Not only am I mad, I'm hot and tired of waiting on Mama. Majors Drugstore, where Grace gets all her medicines, sits on the far corner of the square. Gazing that way, I get an idea.

"Let's go find some air-conditioning to cool off."

Ellie frowns and plants her feet on the sidewalk. "I'm not going anywhere."

"Not *inside*. Let's stroll down to Majors and peer in their window. Someone's bound to open the door sooner or later." I raise my eyebrows up and down.

She gives me a disgusted look and then follows me, knowing I'll keep pestering her until I get my way.

The pharmacy is in the very back of the store, and in the front, Mr. Majors added a small restaurant a few years back. The smell of fresh hamburgers on the grill makes my mouth itch for a taste. Seeing folks inside with ice-filled glasses of Coca-Cola makes me as thirsty as a dirt road.

My eyes light up. "Let's go inside."

"No way, Lillie Mae. I already told you no." Ellie tries so hard to follow the rules. I think she'd have a lot more fun if she didn't worry so much about doing what's right all the time. Besides, Ellie would gulp down a Coca-Cola with me if she got the chance. Unfortunately, her rule-following takes over. "I won't let you talk *me* into gettin' in trouble today. You're in enough trouble on your own."

Feeling a cool breeze, my body starts to relax.

"Hey there, girls." I spin my head around as Mr. Majors holds the door open. "Didn't mean to startle you." He can't tell us apart so he just calls us girls. That happens a lot. People know we're one of the Liles twins, but they can't tell Ellie and me apart any more than two hens in a pen.

"Hello, Mr. Majors." Ellie smiles.

"I saw you girls looking through the window. Can I get you something?"

"No, sir," I say.

"Our Mama told us to wait outside for her," Ellie adds.

"She did, did she? Well, I don't think she's in here right now," he answers.

"She's at the bank," Ellie says.

"Oh. Well, in that case, you girls must need a candy stick."

My mouth waters. I love candy sticks. "No thank you, sir. We don't have any money."

"Then today they are free. Tell me what flavor you want and I'll grab you each a stick."

"Well..." Ellie pauses.

I better hurry and speak up before Ellie decides we need to follow some kind of rule. "We'll have root beer flavor, please."

"Root beer it is. Be right back." He steps inside, and the cool air fades away.

"Lillie, Mama's not gonna like this." Ellie glances toward the bank.

"Why?" I shrug. "We're not doing anythin' wrong."

"She may not see it that way. You know she doesn't like us askin' for things for free." Ellie peers across the street again.

The cool air blows again, moving my sweaty hair away from my face. "Here you go." Mr. Majors hands Ellie and me each a large root beer flavored candy stick wrapped in plastic wrap.

"Thank you." Ripping the plastic wrap off as fast as I can, the candy melts in my mouth.

"You're welcome. Here's one for Grace, too. Y'all take care of that sweet child." He steps back inside, the door closing behind him.

There goes my cool air.

Ellie shoves Grace's stick in the front pocket of her shorts because I'm too busy stuffing my face with candy.

Out of nowhere, Ellie shrieks, shooing at her face. "Bees."

One lands on my candy stick, and I swat at it and miss. The bee stings me, and my candy falls to the ground. Grabbing my hand, I cry out in pain.

"You okay?" Ellie picks up my candy and tries to blow the dirt off of it.

"It hurts." She hands my candy back to me, and I break off the dirty part. Sticking the rest in my mouth, I grumble. "I hate bees."

Ellie laughs. "I told you one day you'd get stung."

Chapter 13 🍋 Mean Girls

AS I STROLL back toward the bank, my hand begins to swell. The feeling of sugar on my tongue is the only thing keeping me calm. Walking past Sawyer's, I peek in the window when the door bursts open.

Violet Holt and her sidekick, Della Grayson, stand in the doorway. Violet wears a light blue dress with white daisies embroidered on the sleeves. Her parents probably bought it at Rich's Department Store. There's one in downtown Atlanta, or so it says on the TV commercial.

Her blonde curls hang in ringlets, and a white ribbon sits on top of her head holding her hair away from her face. She's dressed like Dorothy in *The Wizard of Oz*, but she reminds me of the Wicked Witch of the West.

"Well, if it isn't the poor girls from the pig farm," Violet barks. "I see you haven't had a bath all summer. You smell like the pigs you raise." She scrunches her face making her nose look even more pointed.

"Chickens," I say, continuing to suck on my candy stick.

"What did you say to me?" Violet retorts.

"Chickens. We raise chickens, not pigs."

Della lets out a small snicker. Violet puts her hands on her hips and glares at Della.

"Well, it doesn't matter," Violet snaps back. "You still smell like a farm. I don't know why you think you can go into Sawyer's. You can't afford anything in there anyway."

"Who said we were going in there?" I fire back.

"I said, that's who." Violet scowls at me.

I have had enough of the Holt family for one day.

Violet flips her hair off her shoulder and tosses her head to the side. "My daddy says that the farmers are ruining this town. We're never gonna have shopping malls if you farmers block all the developments. Why we have to put up with you poor folks—"

"Your daddy's a bully," I snap, making a loud crunching noise with my candy. "Without us, your daddy wouldn't have money to pay for the ugly clothes you wear."

"Lillie Mae, you better take that back or else," Violet shrieks. She turns as red as a strawberry.

"Or else what, Violet? You gonna go cry to your daddy? I doubt he'll care."

"I can't believe you think you can talk to me this way. I'll see to it that no one pays any attention to you and your smelly sister at school next year."

She means Peachtree Junior High School where Ellie and I will join my brothers. I'm not sure how she thinks she can rule that school since she's never been there, but it's not worth mentioning. Instead, I ignore her and start to walk away. Violet's about to throw a hissy fit because she hates being ignored.

"Don't you walk away from me, poor girls. I wasn't done talking."

Yep. That's a hissy fit.

I whip my head around. "Well, we're done with you. Actually, Violet, why don't you take your highfalutin' self on home now?"

She inhales a large stream of air, and her hand flies to her open mouth. "Never in my life..."

I don't know what else she said because I walked away, grinning ear to ear.

Ellie cracks up. "What's gotten into you today? I've never seen you so brave."

"I don't know. After speaking my mind to Duke, I feel like I can conquer the world."

"Well you better hope Mama and Daddy see it that way," Ellie warns.

Now that I think about it, I'm not sure if it was such a good idea to let my words fall out of my mouth like that again. If Mama finds out....

I don't have time to think about it because as soon as Ellie and I reach her, she glares at us something fierce. Spotting our candy sticks, Mama's eyes grow wide. Before she can ask, Ellie defends me.

"We didn't ask for it. He gave it to us for free. He gave us one for Grace too. See? It's right here in my pocket. He said it was free today."

Mama's eyes narrow. "Who is *he*?"

"Mr. Majors," I say with my mouth full, forgetting to take the candy out. It comes out sounding more like *missir mayor*.

"And what were you doing at Majors Drugstore?"

"We were lookin' in the window," I answer, doing my best to sound like my sweet tea sister.

"Uh huh. And he happened to come out and give you candy for free?" Mama doesn't believe a word we are saying.

"I swear Mama."

"Lillie Mae, we do not swear."

I look at my feet. "Yes, ma'am."

"She's tellin' the truth, Mama," Ellie interrupts. "Mr. Majors really did come outside and give us a candy stick for free. I promise you that's the honest truth."

"Alright, well, enough about this. We are about to walk into Sawyer's, and candy is not allowed. Put it away for later. And Lillie Mae, for goodness sakes, keep your mouth shut this time."

Biting off the tip of the stick, I fill my mouth. That's about the only way it's going to stay shut. Violet and Della are no longer in front of Sawyer's. Even with a mouth full of candy, I'm not sure I could hold my tongue if Violet says one more nasty thing to me today.

Ellie and I carry the baskets of vegetables to the back of the store. I wince as the straw scratches against my bee sting.

"Now remember girls," Mama warns. "Don't touch a thing."

Chapter 14 ✽ Giggling Fit

THE FRONT of Sawyer's is my favorite part of the store. I'm surrounded by statues, clocks, colorful artwork on the wall, and jewelry. Lots and lots of beautiful jewelry.

I'm drawn to the sparkling earrings, even though we can't afford them. Daddy says the things in Sawyer's are for looking, not for buying. Mama sure would look beautiful with red or green stones in her ears.

While Mama talks to Mr. Rumsfeld, a shiny fabric near the jewelry case catches my eye. Mama told me not to touch anything, and since she's busy, I'm hoping she won't notice. Putting it up to my face, I rub the silky, smooth scarf across my cheek.

"Lillie Mae, what are you doin'?"

I jump to the ceiling. Ellie caught me. "Please don't tell Mama. I couldn't help myself. Everything in here is so beautiful."

"I know," Ellie whispers, glancing around for Mama. "I touched the scarves too." She giggles, and then I do too. We both know what's coming. We're about to have a twin giggling fit.

Ellie tries to suppress her laughter and it comes out sounding like as a snort. My head falls back in laughter. My giggles have left my body and I can't get them back. Pretty soon, we cause such a ruckus, Mama heads straight for us.

When Mama is mad, her face contorts into a tiny smile. This time, though, the smile is missing. *Uh oh.*

"Girls, wait outside please." It comes out sounding nice like sweet maple syrup, but Mama's holding her tongue because she's in public. It's what southern women do.

Outside, Ellie and I lean against the store window. We laugh until tears flow down our cheeks. When Mama walks out, she doesn't say a word. She points toward the truck. Climbing up into the cab, no one speaks.

After several minutes, I speak up. "I'm sorry, Mama."

"I know, Lillie Mae." She stares straight ahead.

"Are you mad at me?"

"Disappointed is more like it." She doesn't look at me.

Being disappointed is even worse, and I don't know what to say. We drive in silence, and I wish we could turn on the radio to see if "We Are Family" is playing. Although the drive home from Sawyer's only takes a few minutes, it feels like hours.

Ellie finally gets up the courage to speak. "Why didn't you marry Mr. Rumsfeld, Mama?"

Mama glances at her in surprise. "Just because you are friends with a boy, Ellie, doesn't mean you love him and want to marry him. You should love the person you marry. It works better that way."

"I think I'm gonna marry a prince," Ellie says.

Mama raises one eyebrow. "Interesting. What about you, Lillie? Who do you think you'll marry?"

"I don't ever want to get married."

"Why on earth not?" Mama asks.

"Because if all boys are mean, like my brothers, I think I'll pass."

Mama chuckles, despite her disappointment in me. "Well, I certainly think when the time comes, the right one will not be mean to you."

I sure wish that laughter would have continued. When we get home, Daddy lets me have it. He's more upset about me being disrespectful to Duke than the giggling fit.

"Don't ever talk to Duke Holt that way, you hear me, Lillie Mae? He's not someone to mess with."

"Yes, sir," I answer, hanging my head. "But he's a horrible person, Daddy."

"You think I don't know that? That's why I'm upset with you for crossing him."

"So..." I hesitate before continuing. "You did know him, before this summer I mean?"

There's something in Daddy's expression that I don't recognize. "Yes."

"How do you know him?"

"It was a long time ago. It doesn't matter now. What matters is that you need to be respectful to adults, even if they don't deserve it."

"Why should I be nice to someone who is stealing land from our friends?" My eyes flood with tears.

"Because I said so. And because it's the right thing to do." Daddy puts his arm around me and lets out a long puff of air like he'd been holding his breath.

"I swear to ya, Daddy. I'm not tryin' to be bad. I'm tryin' to help."

"That's the thing. You don't need to help. You need to let me worry 'bout this kind of thing." He pulls me around to face him, but I can't look him in the eye. "Look at me, Lillie Mae." Not moving my chin, I slowly move my eyes upward. Meeting his gaze, he continues. "There's a lot of things that go on that you don't need to concern yourself with. You need to stay out of this mess, ya hear me?"

"Yes, sir."

In the end, I lose my privilege to play baseball in the evenings with my brothers and sisters. Again. And tonight, I'll be eating supper in my room all by myself.

Right before bed, there's a slight knock on the door. Lifting my head off the pillow, Jimmy stands in the doorway. "Hey."

"Hey." I look away not wanting him to know that I've been crying.

"Yeah, so, I just wanted to say..." He scratches the top of his head. "Well, sometimes ya have to stand up for what's right. What I'm tryin' to say is, I'm proud of you."

Chapter 15 🍋 The Secret

A FEW NIGHTS later, and not even one minute into supper, Ellie and I start a twin giggling fit. Again. Mama gives us a disapproving look, and Daddy's fork hitting the plate creates a clanging vibration.

"Oh no you don't, girls." Mama's tone is stern.

"Sorry, Mama," Ellie says, glancing at me. I look down at my lap to keep myself from laughing.

Daddy sits back in the chair, rubbing his hands over his swollen belly. "Delicious spaghetti sauce, Ruth."

"Uh, huh," Pappy agrees. "Delicious. I'm as full as a tick."

Ellie and I both cover our mouths to suppress the giggles.

"What's so funny?" Daddy glances between us.

"Mama put Lillie's squished squash in the spaghetti sauce. That's why it tastes so good." Ellie bursts into laughter.

Daddy's laugh is so loud, it nearly busts my eardrum. "You kids help clean up. Then y'all go play ball."

Loading the last of the dishes into the dishwasher, Ellie and I wander outside. I'm so tired my bones ache. In fact, I'm too tired for baseball. Now that's a first.

The grownups sit in the rocking chairs, so I collapse dead-tired on the front porch. The sun fades in the distance, casting red streaks in the sky. I hear the cicadas in the yard chirping in harmony.

Daddy rubs the stubble on his unshaven chin. "Today was the longest gasoline line I've seen," he says. "There were probably thirty trucks lined up."

Mama looks up. "Did you get any?"

"Nope. They ran out."

Pappy sits in the rocking chair next to Meemaw, who knits a blanket for Grace out of purple yarn. "Did you see the news?" Pappy asks. "In California, folks are parkin' their cars the night before and leavin' them in line so they can get gas on their rationed day."

"Yeah, I heard," Daddy answers. "Georgia's thinkin' 'bout doing the same thing. Sign at the filling station said two dollars and six cents a gallon. It's absurd."

Pappy shakes his head. "Um, um. That's the reason President Carter has officially named this an oil shortage."

Mama lets out a long sigh. "It's hard to believe that what's happening over there can affect us so much."

I pick up bits and pieces. Something about a man far away leaving his country, but what that has to do with gas in Georgia, I have no idea.

The noise of the cicadas in perfect rhythm has me mesmerized. It's crazy what a ruckus insects can cause. Every once in a while, when the noise stops for no apparent reason, I imagine one of the girl bugs getting tired of talking to a boy bug who isn't paying any attention to her.

The sudden silence makes me look up. Tears form in the corners of Mama's eyes. Daddy wraps his arm around her shoulder. I can't imagine why gasoline would make Mama want to cry.

"Lillie Mae," Meemaw says, interrupting my thoughts. "Let's you and me go for a little walk." She sets the blanket she's knitting on the rocking chair and tugs me by the arm.

"I don't wanna get up. I'm tired," I groan.

Daddy nods his head toward Pappy's house. "Go on, Lillie Mae. A little walk will do ya some good."

I start to protest, but the look on Daddy's face says it isn't a suggestion. Lifting my tired, aching bones off the porch floor, Meemaw slips her arm through mine and gives me a gentle nudge. I drag my feet down the stairs as if I'm eighty instead of eleven.

"Let's go see if we can find those hard candies you like."

Meemaw keeps candy in a clear Mason jar locked away in a cabinet. She claims she has to hide them from Pappy. I think she really hides them from herself so she won't eat them all in one sitting.

Ellie's ears perk up when she hears the word candy and she follows me. Pappy strolls somewhere behind, and I want to reach the candy jar before he does.

Racing into Meemaw's kitchen, I climb onto her white Formica countertop and reach for the jar. Sticking my head into the cabinet and checking each shelf, it's not there.

"Meemaw," I holler. Whipping my head around, Pappy stands behind me holding the jar, grinning ear to ear. "Oh, Pappy."

He chuckles. "I moved it last week." He winks at me. "Don't tell Meemaw."

"I heard that, William," Meemaw shouts from the porch.

Pappy and I giggle. "Here ya go." He hands me three pieces from the jar, and I stuff all of them in my mouth. "Whoa, slow down. Your cheeks are gonna explode."

Pappy has been saying the same thing to me ever since I was a little girl, and I laugh every time. The image of my cheeks exploding is hilarious.

"Maybe y'all ought to stick to just one piece," Meemaw complains, strolling into the family room.

Ellie sits on the blue couch. On the end table in a shiny gold frame is a picture of my parents when they were young. Picking it up, I gaze at the two faces staring back at me.

"Where was this picture taken, Meemaw?"

Meemaw takes the picture from my hands and stares at it for several seconds before answering. "At the high school. Right after a ball game."

"Will you tell me the story again, how Mama and Daddy met?" Meemaw knows I've heard this story before and that I'm stalling, hoping for another piece of candy.

"Come on. Let's you and me sit down with Ellie." She lowers herself to the blue couch. "You already know the story."

Crunching my candy, my aching body slithers onto the soft fabric. "I wanna hear it again," I lie. The truth is, I'm playing detective hoping to find out how Daddy knew Duke.

Meemaw sighs. "This picture was taken right after the high school baseball team won their division and was headin' to the state championship. It was one of the best games Tommy Ray ever pitched.

"Coach said he'd get a scholarship if he could get his grades up. But your daddy was more interested in makin' Ruth happy than going to college." She pauses and looks at the picture. "Boys all over the county wanted to date your mama."

"Did Duke like my Mama?" I blurt out.

Meemaw eyes me suspiciously, her face filled with surprise. "How did you know your mama and Duke knew each other?"

"Daddy told me," I lie again. What he actually said was that *he* knew Duke, but this is what a good detective has to do to get to the truth.

"Oh, I see. What else did he tell you?"

"Nothin'." I shrug. "Just that Duke isn't someone to mess with."

"Hum," she says to herself.

"So, did he like my Mama?"

She doesn't answer me at first. "Yes," she finally says. "Yes, he did."

Ellie crosses her legs and tucks them underneath her. "Did Mama like him back?"

"Oh, no. She only had eyes for your daddy. When baseball season started, Ruth sat on those bleachers every practice and every game. I ain't never seen anything like those two in all my life. They never got tired of each other. Sometimes Ruth's mother would make them stay apart 'cause she wanted Ruth to go to college."

"To be a teacher," I interrupt.

"Exactly, and she would have if—"

"Her parents hadn't died?" Ellie interrupts.

We knew this part of the story. Mama was only eighteen-years-old when her parents were killed at a train crossing.

Meemaw fiddles with her fingernails. "Yep. Saddest thing I've ever seen. Did your Mama ever tell ya that she took classes at the junior college after her parents passed, while living with her aunt?"

"No," Ellie answers.

"Yep, sure thing. Ruth always did think she could do it all. Her plan was to go to college to become a teacher and then marry your daddy."

"So, what happened?" Ellie asks.

"Jimmy and Jesse were born—that's what. Then y'all came, and well, ya know the rest."

What I didn't know was that Mama gave up going to college for me. Maybe that's why she feels the need to correct my grammar.

I'm trying my best to be a good detective, but Meemaw sure isn't making my job easy. She still hasn't answered my most important question.

"What happened between Duke and my Daddy? Back then I mean?" I wait for Meemaw to answer.

She doesn't say anything at first. She looks down at her feet and continues to fiddle with her nails. "It was a long time ago, girls."

"That's what Daddy always says." I raise my voice. "What is it y'all don't want us to know?"

"There's a lot you don't need to know," Meemaw barks. "Sometimes the past just needs to stay in the past."

"I don't understand," I say. "If Daddy and Mama knew Duke in high school, why do they hate each other so much now?"

Meemaw sighs. "You ain't gonna let this go, are ya, Lillie Mae?"

I shake my head.

Meemaw lets out a long breath of air. "Duke was both the star quarterback for the football team and an amazing baseball player. A true athlete, that boy. He could run like the wind. But he didn't come from a good family. Nope, not at all.

"One night, toward the end of baseball season, Tommy Ray took Ruth out on a date to the movies. Afterward, they went to a party at the old Cleveland barn. Y'all know where it used to be?"

"Sure," Ellie says. "Over near Sarah and Mary Olivia's house."

"Yep, that's the one. It's been torn down, but back then, young people went there for parties. Pappy and I didn't like it much. Bad things happened there, and we worried Tommy Ray might get caught up in it.

"He and your mama, they were both good kids. Unfortunately, not all the kids at the party were so good. Tommy Ray was outside with some friends when he realized he hadn't seen Ruth in a while. He figured she was off with her friends and he went lookin' for her." Meemaw stops.

"What, Meemaw? What happened?" I ask.

"What happened to who?" Pappy's voice startles me and I jump off the couch. "Didn't mean to scare you."

"Well, girls, it's getting late." Meemaw stands up.

"But Meemaw," I protest.

"Not now, Lillie." She nods toward Pappy. "Let's get you home."

"IT DOESN'T make sense," I gripe the next morning. "There's something Meemaw's leaving out." Being a good detective is hard work, and so far, I haven't learned very much.

Ellie stares me straight in the eye. "Lillie Mae, you don't know when to quit. You're gonna stick your nose in a bee's nest, get stung, then blame the bee. You've already been stung once this summer."

Ignoring her comment about the bee sting, I yank zucchini from the vine. My mind tries to fit the pieces of the puzzle together. "It doesn't explain why Duke wants our land all these years later."

"You know he wants to build a shopping mall, and Daddy says we have some of the best land around."

"I don't buy it," I answer, dropping zucchini into my bag. "There's something else going on, and I'm gonna find out what it is."

"Okay, Sour Lemon. When are you gonna learn? Meemaw said the past needs to stay in the past." Ellie grits her teeth.

"Whatever."

"I'm warning you, Lillie. You're gonna get stung. Bad this time."

Humph. Now I'm mad. Ellie and her rule following. We'll see who is sour when I find out the secret my parents are hiding from us.

Ellie and I help Mama cut carrots and peel potatoes for supper. A hint of something spicy drifting from the oven makes my stomach growl.

Daddy stands at the sink, washing his hands. "Gasoline was over two dollars a gallon again today, Ruth."

Mama exhales. "I think just last year it was around a dollar sixty-seven. If prices keep going up, we're not going be able to afford to put gas in the truck."

"Yep, I know. Earlier today there were cars lined up for miles to get gas. I'm gonna park the truck tonight at the filling station."

Mama sets the chicken on the table and whips her head around. "Leave it overnight?"

"Got to, or they'll run out."

Everyone sits at the round kitchen table waiting to eat. We know better than to interrupt. George sticks his finger in the creamed potatoes and licks it. Ellie slaps his hand.

"Ouch. Stop it, Ellie," he barks.

"Hush, George," Jesse whispers.

My parents don't even notice. They continue their conversation like we're not even there. My stomach growls again.

"Do you think that's safe, Tommy Ray?" Mama asks.

"I don't see what choice we have. If you're not in line by seven a.m., you don't get gas. Truck's near empty as it is. Reckon we ought to eat now," he says, as if noticing us for the first time.

Daddy says the blessing and adds a little prayer about gasoline. I can't understand why grownups get so upset about certain things like gas when there are more pressing matters like the secrets they're keeping from me.

"I'll get Pappy to take me," Daddy says to Mama. "We'll park our truck tonight, then tomorrow, we'll switch."

After supper, Daddy turns the TV to the news station. The top story of the day is the gas shortage. The announcer says filling stations all across Georgia are running out of gas before closing time.

"Mama. Do you think Daddy will let me ride with him tonight to park the truck?" I'm hoping to do some detective work and find out more about that secret he's hiding.

"I don't know, Lillie Mae. You can go ask him."

Setting the dried plates in the cupboard, I leave the kitchen and plop down next to Daddy on our yellow flowered couch.

"Hey, Daddy," I say, batting my eyelashes the way I've seen Ellie do it.

"Hey, there." He doesn't even notice. He keeps staring at the TV.

Since batting my eyelashes didn't get his attention, this time, I opt for a sweet voice. "Can I can ride with you and Pappy tonight to park the truck?" I try to sound as sweet as a honeybee.

"I don't see why not, as long as your chores are done."

"Yes, sir, they are."

"Well alright then. Run on outside, and I'll meet you there in a bit."

As we approach the service station, I count three trucks in front of us and four more piling in. The station won't even be open until tomorrow morning. Daddy parks the Chevy in line near the entrance, while Pappy pulls his old Ford off to the side. Leaving the Chevy, Daddy and I climb into Pappy's front seat.

"All these trucks are gonna stay here all night?" I ask.

"Yep. And we gotta be back by five-thirty in the morning."

"I don't understand. Why are the stations running out?"

"It's hard to explain, Lillie Mae." Daddy rolls down his window. "We get our gasoline from countries across the ocean. So, when they have problems, we have problems too."

Pappy's arm hangs out the truck. "Some states are followin' California and goin' to ration days."

"What's a ration, Pappy?"

"Means you can only get gas on certain days."

"What if you run out of gas before it's your day?"

Daddy gazes out the window. "Well, that's the problem. Sometimes you do."

Now's my chance to turn on my detective skills. "So, if we can't get gas, can we still keep our farm?"

Daddy stares at me. "We'll keep our farm one way or the other. Don't ya worry 'bout that." Before glancing away, he and Pappy exchange a troublesome look.

My mind swirls. I'm starting to put the pieces of this mysterious puzzle together.

Chapter 17 🍋 Bee's Nest

DADDY WAKES me so early the next morning, the rooster doesn't even want to crow yet. My brothers gobble their breakfast as Daddy mixes cream and sugar into his coffee.

Still half asleep, I pour milk on my cereal, and it splashes Daddy's hand. "Wake up, Lillie Mae. We got to get goin'."

"Yes, sir," I murmur, wiping the table with my napkin and shoving cereal in my mouth.

"Lloyd's coming by this morning, boys, to pick up the chickens. Y'all need to get them ready while I'm gone." Lloyd Eades works for Silo Farms. He's worked with Daddy since I was born.

When we arrive at the station, cars and trucks are lined up for what looks like miles all along Highway Nine. Thank goodness we were one of the first in line last night or we might not have gotten any gas.

An oil truck sits by the pumps. Daddy hops out of Pappy's truck and waves over his shoulder. "See y'all back at the house."

"See ya, Daddy." I face Pappy. "How long will he have to sit here?"

"Depends. Maybe an hour. Maybe two."

"You gonna bring your truck back up here tonight?"

"Yep. Have to."

I want to ask more, like why he and Daddy exchanged that look last night, but Pappy doesn't say anything else. We ride in silence for a while before I get up the courage to ask what is really on my mind.

"Meemaw told me about Duke."

"Yeah?" he says, raising his eyebrows. He doesn't offer any information.

Careful not to be too obvious, I continue my investigation. "What really happened with him and Daddy back then?"

Pappy sits silently, and for a minute, I think he didn't hear me. Then, just barely above a whisper, he answers. "I suppose it's time you knew. Maybe then you'll understand what your daddy's been tryin' to teach ya." His eyes shoot toward me. I don't know what lesson I'm supposed to be learning, but I have a feeling I'll know soon. He stays quiet again making me wonder if this is all he plans to tell me. Then, he whispers. "So what'd Meemaw tell ya?"

"That Daddy took Mama to a party at the old Cleveland barn, and Daddy went looking for her. That's it. That's all she told me." I fully expect him to tell me the rest of the story, but he stays quiet. His eyes never leave the road, and his knuckles turn white from gripping the steering wheel. Clearing my throat, my detective work must continue. "Well, did he find her? What happened?"

"Yep. He found her in the barn." He stares straight ahead. "Duke liked your mama and was always tryin' to get her to go out on a date with him. Made Tommy Ray real mad. That night,

Duke was tryin' to kiss your mama, and when Tommy Ray saw it, he went crazy. The two boys got in a fistfight. Both boys went home that night with black eyes." Pappy shakes his head. "Fightin' ain't a good idea."

"Jimmy and Freddie got in a fist fight once, and they're still friends."

Pappy glances my way. "Jimmy's a lot like your daddy. Got himself a temper."

"How was Daddy's fight any different? And why aren't they still friends?"

"When Duke punched Tommy Ray, he hurt his shoulder real bad. Duke had to miss practice the next day. When the coach found out why, he pulled Duke and your daddy out of the game that week to teach them both a lesson. The team lost the game, and it cost them the championship."

"Wait. Weren't they only in eleventh grade?"

Pappy nods.

"So they could've played the next year, right?"

"They did, but I reckon Duke never did play too good after that. Couldn't throw the ball for nothin'. Football team lost nearly every game that year. Duke blamed your daddy, even though it really wasn't his fault.

"As for Tommy Ray, well, he learned his lesson. He asked Duke to forgive him, but Duke wouldn't hear of it. Said your daddy ruined his career. Duke said one day he'd get revenge. And, well, he's been trying to get back at your daddy ever since."

"Is that why he's tryin' to steal our land?" I whisper. A single tear escapes my eye unnoticed and makes its way down my cheek.

Pappy gives me a sad expression. "Maybe I shouldn't have told you all that, Lillie Mae."

"No, it's okay, Pappy," I lie. "I wanted to know." At least I think I did. Now, I'm not so sure.

When I get home, Ellie takes one look at me and knows exactly what happened. "You stuck your nose in the bee's nest, didn't you?"

I stare down at my feet. "What do I do now?"

"You do what you should've done before, Lillie. You let it go."

Twirling my hair around my finger, I cross one arm over my chest. "Daddy thinks I should be respectful to people, even when they don't deserve it. I don't know how to do that."

Ellie shrugs. "Anyone can change. That's what forgiveness is for."

"Duke didn't forgive."

She smiles. "He chose not to. It was, and still is, his choice. We all get to choose whether we love or hate. I just choose to love is all."

Lying in bed that night, my mind tries to make sense of what Ellie said. How it's my choice to love those who don't deserve it. I guess that's the lesson I'm supposed to be learning. Daddy's been trying to teach me about forgiveness.

Chapter 18 🍋 Crushed

SECRETS ARE a funny thing. Sometimes, it's good for them to come to the surface. But other times, like the secret about Duke and my parents, it may be best to leave them buried.

As many times as I've spied on the grownups, this is the first time I've felt a sting. And let me tell you, it hurts. Now that I've discovered the truth about Duke, I'm even more convinced that he wants to steal our land. I know who to go to for help, but it will have to wait. Right now, there are more pressing matters. Like taming my horrible hair a few minutes before we leave for church.

Every Saturday night, I wash my hair and sleep in pink sponge curlers. This morning, when I took out the curlers, my hair was higher than our barn roof. Thank goodness Ellie has some sort of smelly goop she concocted out of garden vines to calm it down.

"What in the world is this stuff?" I bark, touching my hair.

"You don't wanna know," Ellie answers. "It's one of Meemaw's old recipes she got from her mama. Now quit touching."

"It smells worse than D house," I complain, pinching my nose. "I don't think anyone's gonna want to be near me."

Ellie rolls her eyes. "The smell will fade. At least I think it will. That's what Meemaw said."

My eyes go wide. "You mean you've never used this before?"

"No. Calm down. It'll be fine."

"Easy for you to say. You're not the one who smells like rotten eggs mixed with chicken poop."

Ellie lets out a loud puff of air. "Do you think Cute Boy knows your birthday is comin' up?"

I whip my head around. "Where did that come from? No, he doesn't know about my birthday, and he isn't gonna care if I smell like this."

"Would ya hush about the smell? I'm serious. I think we should talk to him today."

"We?" I ask, raising my eyebrows.

"Why not? You've been wantin' to talk to him. Maybe I should help you along."

It's true. I have looked for Cute Boy every week at church. He hasn't been back since the beginning of summer.

"Don't you dare, Ellie." My face flushes, and my stomach flips.

She tilts her head to one side. "He may want to know about your birthday. In case he wants to get you a present."

"Stop it. That's ridiculous," I gripe, gritting my teeth together.

"Hmm? What did you say? I didn't hear you."

"Ellie," I shriek, chasing her around the room.

She giggles. "Lillie Mae, you're gonna mess up your hair."

I plop onto her bed. Ellie strolls to our closet and pulls out a yellow and white flowered dress. "Here. Wear this one." Slipping on the dress, I tug the white panty hose onto my legs. The white pumps are the final straw.

Staring at myself in the mirror, my lips curve downward. "Don't you think this is a bit much, Ellie?"

"Of course it is," she replies. "But you wanna make a good impression, don't ya?"

I'm not sure what impression I'll be making considering it's one hundred degrees with one hundred percent humidity. My smelly curls are already starting to frizz.

When we arrive at church, my head moves side to side watching for Cute Boy. Spotting him across the aisle, he looks up and catches me staring. I'm so embarrassed, I jerk my head in the other direction feeling my face heat up. Jimmy pushes my shoulder making me lose my balance.

"Move, Lillie Mae, so I can get in," Jimmy barks.

Ellie sits down next to me and whispers in my ear a little too loudly. "That's him, isn't it?"

"Shh." I don't want my brothers to hear.

"He's cute. And he smiled at you."

"He did?" My face beams.

"Of course he did because I made you look beautiful today." She giggles.

Cute Boy catches me peeking again. This time I smile back.

When Pastor Eddie dismisses us from the service, Ellie and I bolt to the same row in Sunday school where we always sit. Using the church bulletin, I fan my cheeks. Ellie drops down in the chair next to me. When I turn to look for Mary Olivia, Cute Boy is right in front of my face.

"Hey," he says.

"Hey." I exhale, surprised I could speak.

"Is this seat taken?"

"Uh, no." I lie. Actually, it's Mary Olivia's. Always has been. What she'll say when she gets here is anyone's guess.

He sits down, neither one of us speaking. My face heats up again, and I wonder if I have red, splotchy cheeks. *Gulp.*

When Mary Olivia marches to our row, she gives me a funny look. I shrug my shoulders, and she sits somewhere else without commenting. *That's a first.*

"Good morning," Miss Marsh says. "Let's get started. Today we are covering the story of Joseph and his coat of many colors. Does anyone know who gave him the colorful coat?"

Jesse raises his hand before anyone else can even think about what Miss Marsh asked. "His father gave it to him." Jesse grins.

I roll my eyes.

"Yes, Jesse, that's correct."

As Miss Marsh continues teaching, everyone lets Jesse answer all the questions. I kind of feel sorry for him.

Although his heart is in the right place, he just doesn't know when to stop talking.

I don't hear much of what Miss Marsh says after that. I'm too distracted with Cute Boy inches from me. Of course, I already know the story of Joseph and the coat of many colors, considering I've been in church since I was born. When the lesson is over, my mind swirls at the thought of talking to him. It's kind of funny that I still don't know his real name.

"Bye," he says, waving.

Lost in thought, I stare at him. As he walks out the door, Ellie elbows me in the arm. "You could've at least waved."

"I know. I froze."

Jesse barges in on our conversation. "Hey. Saw Wyatt Jackson sat next to you today. You know him?"

Wyatt. That's a nice name. I take a deep breath. "Wyatt? Um, no. Seen him around is all. Why? Do you know him?" I ask, acting like I don't care.

"Not really. Moved here last year from a nearby town. Don't rightly know which one. He's alright I guess. Doesn't say much."

"Well, that explains it," I complain under my breath.

"Explains what?"

"Nothin'."

He shrugs, then leans in close, whispering in my ear. "His daddy's a builder, and I'll give you one guess who he works for." My eyes widen, and Jesse frowns. "Duke Holt."

A long puff of air escapes from my lips. "Oh, great," I groan.

Jesse and I stroll across the parking lot toward the truck when Wyatt shouts my name. Jesse shoots me a look, a question mark in his eye, as Jimmy watches from the truck. Wyatt never does get the chance to say whatever it is he came to say.

"Wyatt. Come on, son. Time to go." His daddy stands in the parking lot with his arms folded across his chest and a scowl on his face.

Wyatt turns around without uttering a word. He peeks over his shoulder and gives me a slight wave.

Managing a slight smile, I whisper under my breath. "Bye."

Wyatt's father puts his arm around him and leads him to their car. "Leave that family alone, Wyatt." He isn't whispering, that's for sure. I bet the entire church congregation heard what he said from inside the building. "You don't have any business hangin' around them. They can't afford the land they live on, but they won't sell to Duke's investor. Sounds stupid to me." Mr. Jackson glances over his shoulder.

My legs turn to stone. Then, everything looks watery as I race to the truck.

Sometimes kids at school say stupid stuff like, "Your family is poor because y'all have too many twins," or "Y'all could have nicer things if your parents weren't so poor."

Funny thing is, most of them are poor farm kids too, so it's never really bothered me. Until today. This time is different somehow. Maybe it's because I have a crush on Wyatt. Or *had* a crush.

Whoever said, "Sticks and stones may break my bones, but words will never hurt me" was wrong. Words do hurt.

Jesse hops into the back of the truck where my knees are pulled up to my chest. My arms hug my knees, and my head is buried in my lap. "Don't pay them any attention, Lil. That isn't about you. Some folks are mean when they don't understand someone else."

"Stupid jerk," Jimmy growls, jumping into the back. "I'll take care of that next time I see that boy."

"No, Jimmy," I plead through my tears. I don't want them to get in a fist fight.

"Why not? He deserves it."

"It's not Wyatt, Jimmy," Jesse blurts out. "It's his daddy. He doesn't know better."

"You always say that, Jesse." Jimmy's fingers curls into a fist, and his face flushes. "The thing is, he *does* know better. One day, I'm gonna get out of this town."

When we pull up to the house, my legs propel me out of the Chevy, and I head straight to my room. Falling down on Ellie's bed, the familiar squeak of the mattress brings me comfort. Grace and Ellie sit next to me.

"It's okay, Lillie Mae." Grace pats my back. I know she's trying to make me feel better.

Ellie holds my hand. "Don't cry, Lillie. That's what I'm supposed to do. You're the tough one, remember?"

Mama walks in my room, closing the door behind her. She strokes my back like she did when I was little and had a bad dream.

"Lillie Mae," she says slowly. "Sometimes folks don't understand our family so they say horrible things without thinking. I love you, and you're my special girl, no matter what anyone else says." She rubs my back. "You're special to God, too. He created you exactly how He wanted you. He made you part of this family at this particular time. And God doesn't make mistakes."

I try to catch my breath between tears. "It hurt my feelings. Wyatt and his daddy don't even know me. How can they not like me?"

Mama pulls at my chin, making me look her in the eye. "This isn't about you, Lillie Mae, and I don't want you to ever think it is. You are special, and no one can take that away from you." I sit up and hug Mama as she wipes my tears with her hands. "Lillie Mae, you're trying to worry about too many things. You're just a child. Let me do the worrying for you instead of the other way around, okay? Can you do that?"

"Yes, Mama," I reply, feeling confused. I'm not really a child, but I'm not an adult either. "I thought I liked Wyatt, ya know."

"I know. Ellie told me." She smiles. "I think Wyatt might like you, too." There's a sparkle in her eye.

A smile fills my face, and my tears dry up. At least for now.

Chapter 19 ☀ July Fourth

THE FOURTH of July is my favorite holiday. Well, my second favorite after my birthday, that is. Every summer since I can remember, the town throws a big parade right down Main Street. It's a celebration not to be missed. After the parade, my family takes a big picnic to the lake and spends the day swimming and watching fireworks at dark.

Although I like everything about the celebration, the thing I look forward to the most is drinking a bottle of Coca-Cola. In fact, it's the only day all year that I am allowed to have Coke.

Mama is big on traditions. Some traditions, like family meetings, I'd just as soon drown in the county creek. Yet when it comes to Coca-Cola, I'm tradition's biggest fan.

Despite our struggles, Mama wants today to be special. We even got the day off from work, and I slept until my eyes wouldn't stay shut any longer.

"Well, good morning." Mama stares at Ellie and me. "I never dreamed when I said you two could sleep late, that it would be *this* late." She points to the clock on the wall.

Grace stands on a chair covered in flour, and Ellie tickles her tummy. "Grace, did you paint yourself this morning? You're covered in white paste."

"No, silly. I'm helping Meemaw with the fried chicken."

"I thought maybe we were gonna fry you up instead," I tease.

"Lillie Mae, you're so crazy," Grace responds. Ellie and I giggle.

"Oh, no, you don't girls." Mama wags her finger in front of my face. "Don't you start that giggling fit. We have lots of work to do if you want to get to the lake before dark."

"Mama," Grace interrupts. "It's not even close to dark out yet."

"It's a figure of speech, Grace." Mama winks at me. "Lillie and Ellie, get your breakfast out of the refrigerator. I put some bacon away for you. Then, I need your help."

"Yes, ma'am."

"Edith. Will you pour some flour onto a plate for Lillie Mae?"

"Sure thing," Meemaw answers. "Here you go, Lillie Mae. Here's you a plate."

She sets the plate in front of me, splashing flour on my shorts. As I bend over to wipe it off, I put my face too close to the plate, and white flour sprays everywhere, including my face. Meemaw shakes her head at the sight of me. "Grace. Now we match," I laugh.

Rolling each piece of chicken in the flour, Meemaw drops it into the frying pan and cooks it up nice and brown. I love Meemaw's fried chicken. Next to Coke and candy, fried chicken may be my next favorite food.

The smell of chicken sizzling in a pan of oil makes my mouth water with excitement. When the chicken's done, I wrap each piece in kitchen towels to keep them from drying out. Grace packs the homemade pickles we made last week from our garden cucumbers and places them in the picnic basket next to the chicken.

Baskets in hand, Ellie follows me outside with cornbread, potato salad, and coleslaw. My brothers load blankets, swim towels, and fishing poles. They love spending the day fishing. The lake has the best catfish you will ever taste.

Pappy carries a large ice chest toward our truck, and we all know what that means.

"Coke!" I shout.

Mama throws her hands in the air. "Of course. It's tradition."

Thank goodness for traditions. "I just thought since—"

"It wouldn't be Fourth of July without it," Mama interrupts. I squeeze her so hard, she falls backward. "Whoa, Lillie Mae. You about knocked me off my feet. Go thank Pappy. This is his doing."

George hangs on Pappy, trying to open the ice chest. "Whoa, slow down there boy," Pappy grumbles.

"I wanna see them." George bounces up and down.

"Ya will. Once we get to the lake. Go on now, and lemme get this loaded."

He sets the ice chest down in the bed of the truck. Sneaking up behind him, my arms stretch around his waist. "You're the best Pappy I have."

"Well, my word. I ain't never seen such a fuss over soda pop in all my life." He acts mad, but he's really teasing.

Ellie and I dash to our room to get dressed. "Lillie, do you like this one on me?" Ellie holds up a red striped swimsuit and twirls around in circles.

"I like the blue one on you better."

"Okay. Then I'll wear blue. Which one are you gonna to wear?"

I don't want to wear either one. "I'm not sure. I think maybe the blue one looks best on me, too."

"It's fine with me if you wanna match."

Ellie buckles my swimsuit top for me. It's really not the bathing suit that's got me so upset. It's the fact that my body is changing, and I don't like it.

Ellie gets in my face and does her eyebrow up and down thing to try to get me to laugh. "What's botherin' ya?"

"Nothin. We better get goin." Looking away, I tug a pair of shorts on over my bathing suit.

"I know there's somethin' you're not telling me. I can tell."

"It's nothin'." Ellie stares at me with her big, brown eyes and wiggles her eyebrows up and down again. "Okay, I'll tell ya. Promise me you won't get mad."

"I pinky promise." Ellie grabs my pinkie finger into hers.

"I don't like the way I look. No matter what bathing suit you put on, you look beautiful. When I try the same thing, I don't look like you."

"Yes, you do. You're my identical twin, Lillie. So like it or not, you do look like me."

"Well, sort of. My body is...well, changing."

"It's supposed to." She chuckles. "Besides, I think you are the most beautiful twin in the whole wide world."

"You have to say that 'cause I am *your* twin," I say, shaking my head.

"True. But I don't *have* to say it. I could say you're as ugly as Jimmy."

A grin streaks across my face.

"Load 'em up," Daddy shouts. "Let the parade begin."

Daddy says the same thing every year, and you'd think we would all roll our eyes. Instead, we whoop and holler. Pappy drives his Ford with Mama and Meemaw sitting beside him. Daddy climbs in the back of the truck with us kids. Ever since he was five-years-old, Daddy has ridden in the back of Pappy's truck to the parade. Another one of our family traditions.

Crowds fill the square, so we park a couple of blocks down. Jimmy hops out before Pappy can park, and Jesse trots off with Billy. I sure hope I don't run into Wyatt.

"Ellie. Lillie Mae. Y'all are in charge of George and Grace today," Mama says. "Stay with them. There's already a crowd forming."

"Yes, ma'am," I answer.

Taking George's hand, we skip to our regular spot on the curb. The Triple Gap High School marching band strolls down the street playing, "You're a Grand Ole' Flag," with folks singing and clapping along.

The float from Sawnee Community Bank drives by next. It's really pretty with dozens of colored flowers. Daddy and Mama look away.

When our church float comes by, my family stands and cheers. Every Fourth of July, one family is picked to ride on the float. Although my family has been waiting for years, we still haven't been picked. Jimmy says there are too many of us and that we might fall off the float. I don't know if that's true or not. All I know is I'd sure like to ride on that float one day.

When the fire engine's siren roars, all the kids cheer because we know what's next. Candy. And lots of it.

Ellie and I chase the fire truck, catching candy as we go. Mary Olivia stands off to the side, and I shout hello. Caught up in all the excitement, I forget to keep an eye on George and Grace.

"Mary Olivia. Do you see George? Or Grace?"

She glances around. "Nope."

"I was supposed to keep an eye on them." There are kids running all over the place, and panic fills the inside of my chest. Suddenly, I can't breathe. "Grace, George!" I shout above the crowd. It's no use. The music is too loud.

Spinning in circles, my eyes scan the crowd. Up the road, I spot Ellie skipping down the street with Grace on one hand and George on the other. I let out a long breath and feel life returning to my lungs.

Grace pounces into me. "Hey, Lillie Mae. Look at how much candy I got." She puts her fists in front of me.

"Y'all scared me half to death. I didn't know where you were," I yell.

"Don't worry, Lillie. I got them. I know you forgot you were supposed to be watching The Twins." She smiles.

Now I feel bad. "I'm sorry, Ellie."

"It's okay. You were havin' fun with Mary Olivia. Here, take George so he can get more candy. He thinks Grace got more than him, and we might have a twin fight later if you don't."

"She did get more than me." George crosses his arms over his chest and sticks out his lower lip.

"Okay, fine. Come on. Let's go chase the truck again." I take George by the hand and run back to the fire engine. He squeals when the fireman hands him a red plastic fire hat.

"Tell him thank you, George."

"Thank you."

"You're welcome," the firefighter shouts above the siren.

George stuffs his pockets with candy, then takes the hat from me and puts it on. "We oh, we oh," he squeals, imitating the siren.

George and I make our way back to the curb. Spotting Mama and Daddy, he lets go of my hand and runs to them. "The fireman gave me a hat."

Daddy pats him on the head and smiles. "Good job, son."

As the parade ends, we head for the truck. Everyone's mouth is full of candy, and George's cheeks look like a squirrel storing nuts.

"That's enough candy, George." Mama sighs. "You're gonna choke yourself."

George tries to say something when a piece of candy flies out of his mouth and hits Billy in the back of the head. Billy whips around and tackles me to the ground. I'm too stunned to say anything.

"Billy," Mama shrieks. "Stop that this instant."

Daddy grabs Billy by the collar and yanks him to the truck. "Don't you ever do that to one of your sisters again. Ya hear me?"

"Yes, sir," Billy answers. "But she threw a piece of candy at my head, and it hurt."

"I did not," I shout back. Jesse helps me up, and I wipe the dirt off my shorts. My dirty hands have scrapes, and there's a tiny bit of blood on my right hand.

"I don't care if she threw a rock at your head. You never hurt a girl. Understood?" Daddy's pupils are dilated.

"Yes, sir." Billy's stomps to the truck.

Daddy faces me. "Lillie Mae. Why would you do such a thing?"

"I didn't, Daddy."

"Then who did?"

"I did," George bellows, through a mouth of crushed up sugar. "I didn't mean to. My mouth got so full, it exploded. That candy came flying out before I could stop it."

Daddy laughs so hard he doubles over, holding onto his belly like he was going to lose his breakfast. Billy jumps down off the truck and pulls George into a headlock, tousling his hair and wrestling with him. My hands hurt, and my pretty shorts are dirty, but the thought of George spitting candy out of his mouth is too much, and the giggles spill out of me.

Climbing into the truck, Billy nudges me. "Sorry, Lillie Mae."

"It's okay."

Daddy leaps up in the bed of the Chevy and stands with his arms open wide. "Well now. Who wants to go to the lake?"

It's about time. That's what I've been waiting for all day.

Chapter 20 🍋 The Lake

THE LAKE IS a few miles up the road, and when we arrive, loads of cars and trucks are already filling the parking lot. Wyatt and his family climb out of their parked car, so I turn away. I won't let anything ruin this day for me.

Nearby, in a large, grassy field, Duke throws a baseball to his son, Joey, barking at him the entire time. Daddy pretends not to notice Duke.

"Not like that. Don't you ever listen? Do it like this, son. There you go. That's how I taught you."

Joey stares at his feet. It's hard to imagine being so mean to your own kid.

"Looks like we got it all unloaded," Mama says. "Y'all can go swim now."

Ellie and I tear off our shorts and T-shirts, revealing our matching bathing suits. Leaping into the lake, the cool water feels good against my sweaty body, even though the scrape on my hand burns. Spying Mary Olivia on the sandy beach, I charge at her.

"Lillie Mae, you got my clothes soaked," she says.

"Get in this lake right now before I throw you in," I yell, pretending to pick her up.

"I'm comin'. I need to blow up my raft. My daddy bought it for us to use today."

"A raft?" A big smile spreads across my face.

"Yeah. We're gonna have so much fun." She blows air into the hole. "Oh, and I made you some cookies. Your favorite, chocolate chip."

"You didn't," I grin.

"I most certainly did," she says between breaths.

"That's why you're my best friend, Mary Olivia."

"I know." She smiles and continues to blow air into the raft.

"Ellie. Over here," Sarah calls.

"Comin'," Ellie shouts back.

Mary Olivia and I don't wait for them. We run to the lake and pile on top of the raft, splashing each other in the face. Ellie and Sarah stand in the sand near the shore. I'd bet my last dollar that Sarah doesn't want to get her hair wet. It's common knowledge that Sarah has a crush on Freddie. Guess she wants to look good for him because her curls are taller than the church steeple.

"Are y'all comin' in or what?" I bark.

"I am," Ellie answers. She dives deep into the water and stays under so long, I start to worry. When Ellie pops out of the water, she sprays me like a mermaid, yanking me off the raft and nearly drowning me. We pretend to fight, but we're really laughing at each other's tangled hair.

"Come on, Sarah," Ellie says, climbing onto the raft. "You're not gonna melt."

"I know. I don't want to get my hair wet. That's all."

I roll my eyes. "I wonder why?" Pretending to look past her at someone on the beach, I say in my sweetest, girlie voice, "Oh hey, Freddie."

Sarah's head spins like the weather vane on top of our barn.

"Tricked ya'," I laugh.

"Lillie Mae, that's not funny," she retorts.

"Yes, it was," Mary Olivia giggles. "You might as well get your hair wet now because it isn't perfect anymore."

"Well, maybe I will," Sarah pouts. She looks around for Freddie. "Okay, I'll come in. Promise you won't splash me?"

"I promise," Ellie says, crossing her fingers behind her back.

As soon as Sarah wades into the water, Ellie, Mary Olivia, and I soak her curly hair. She looks like a cat in a bathtub.

"Don't be mad, Sarah," Ellie begs. "We're just playin'."

For a minute, Sarah looks like she might cry. Then without warning, she flips Ellie off the raft, landing her upside down in the water.

Violet stands on the beach perfectly dry. Why she thought to come to a lake dressed in a lacy blouse with white shorts is beyond me. Her mama shops at Rich's department store in downtown Atlanta. I've never been to Rich's, though I hear it is quite spectacular. You'd think someone with that much money would have enough sense to buy a bathing suit.

"Hi, Violet," Mary Olivia says. "Wanna play on the raft with us?" I shove Mary Olivia in the shoulder. "She isn't gonna come in, Lillie. I'm just pestering her," she says to me.

Violet sneers. "Why would I want to play with a bunch of farm girls?"

"It's called fun," I retort. "You ought to try it sometime."

Violet throws her nose in the air. She seems fond of doing that. "Is this your bath for the month, Lillie Mae?"

Heat rises to my face as I clench my teeth together. I have a good mind to pour buckets of water on her head. The thought of soaking Violet's ridiculous outfit makes me grin.

"Lil-lie. Why are you smilin'?" Ellie knows me too well.

Whispering in Ellie's ear, I tell her my mischievous idea. She looks at me like I have lost my mind. Then, her sweet innocent face curves into a smirk.

"Get her," Ellie screeches. We splash Violet, soaking her down to her panties. Violet shrieks like she caught on fire.

It's the funniest thing I've ever seen. The four of us laugh like we've never laughed before. Violet throws a hissy fit right there in the sand. This will forever be one of my favorite memories.

I've been in the water so long, my fingers shrivel up like raisins. I'm starving half to death and want that bottle of Coca-Cola so bad I can taste it.

Bounding out of the water, my feet tiptoe across the hot sand. Pappy stands at the ice chest popping the tops off the Coke bottles. Each bottle lets out a long, fizzy sound.

Taking a big sip, the bubbles reach all the way down to my bones. The sugar on my tongue makes me grin ear to ear. Seeing Jimmy with his plate full of chicken, I dash to get some before it's all gone. My favorite pieces are the drumsticks because it's like holding a handle while you eat.

"Gracious me, Jimmy," Meemaw barks. "I know you're a growin' boy, but save some chicken for everyone else."

Jimmy already has a drumstick hanging from his lips. "Your fried chicken's the best this side of the Mississippi."

"I don't wanna see your food," I bark. He sticks his tongue out at me. "Gross, Jimmy. Stop."

"I get watermelon first, too." He darts to the bucket and I roll my eyes.

"Let him be, Lillie Mae," Meemaw says. "He's growin' like a weed these days."

"A weed don't have to be so mean," I retort. Peering in the bucket of watermelon, Pappy's booming voice behind me gives me the jitters.

"There's plenty, Lillie Mae," Pappy says. "I saved the best piece for you." He smiles and pulls a piece out from behind his back. Ellie starts to object when Pappy interrupts. "Course I also saved a piece for you, Ellie."

"Thank you, Pappy," I say. "You sure know how to make a girl feel good."

"Yeah. Thanks, Pappy," Ellie agrees.

Taking a big bite, watermelon juice squirts out of my mouth and runs down my chin.

Meemaw shakes her head. "Gracious me, Lillie Mae. Sit down on the blanket. Your gonna spill your chicken."

I try to say, "Yes, ma'am", but it comes out more like, "ez may."

Grace, Ellie, and I sit on a blanket, eating until our stomachs nearly burst. I'm so full, I might float on top of the water.

"Don't forget," Mama reminds us. "Wait thirty minutes before getting back in the water."

Guess I won't be floating after all. Ducks usually hang around this part of the lake, so Ellie grabs some cornbread crumbs and we head down to the beach.

"Ducks!" Grace points to a mama duck near the shore with her ducklings following, all in a row. "I'm gonna name that one Duckie Paddles and I'm gonna look for her every time we come from now on."

Crinkling my nose, I frown. "How are you gonna know which one is which? They're all yellow, and soon they're gonna turn white."

"I will know, Lillie. Duckie Paddles has a fluffy feather right in the middle of her head. I'll always know it's <u>her</u>."

"Alrighty. If you say so," I say, shaking my head.

When we run out of crumbs, I rush back to the blanket to get my Coke bottle out of the ice chest. Taking a big sip, the bubbles sit on my tongue. Then, I gulp down the entire bottle.

Just before dark, my family gathers on the blanket to watch the fireworks show. When I gaze into the star-filled sky, the stars appear as if they go on forever.

"Look," Ellie shouts, making me jump. "It's a shooting star!"

"Well, I'll be. It sure is," Mama answers. "Make a wish."

"Fireworks are startin'," Daddy interrupts. He sits next to Mama and puts his arm around her, kissing her forehead.

The sky lights up with color. White lights explode into red and green. Blue lights turn to yellow falling stars. I wish this moment would last forever.

Chapter 21 🍋 Grace

"ONLY ONE week left," Ellie whispers in my ear. Ellie stands next to my bunk bed making her eyebrows bob up and down on her face. Laughing a bit too loud, we wake up Grace.

"What are y'all laughing at?" she asks, coughing.

"Only one week left till our birthday," Ellie says.

"Why is that funny?"

"It's not," I answer. "Ellie's making her eyebrows go up and down."

Ellie climbs onto Grace's bed and does her eyebrow thing. Grace giggles then coughs.

"What should we wear to our party, Ellie?"

"I think we should wear our pink and white checkered shorts. You wear the pink shirt with the checker pattern on it, and I'll wear the white blouse with lace."

"Okay. That sounds good."

Our party is a spend-the-night get-together at Meemaw and Pappy's house. Meemaw says we can sleep on her floor and watch television after she and Pappy go to bed. Every year, Meemaw makes us the same birthday cake—half vanilla and half chocolate with white icing on top. That way Ellie and I both get our favorite. As Ellie and I stroll to the garden, we talk non-stop about our birthday.

"That's all," cough, cough, "y'all talk about anymore," cough, cough. Grace tries to say something, but between the coughs, it's hard to understand her.

"Slow down, Grace," Ellie says, shooting me a look.

"I'm tired," cough, "of hearing 'bout your birthday." Grace can't catch her breath.

"You feel okay? Sure are coughin' a lot." Ellie drops her gardening gloves in the dirt.

"Do you have your puffer?" I ask.

"Yeah," Grace manages to say between coughs.

"Let's get it out. Try taking two puffs, okay?" I lead her to a spot on the edge of the woods where we sit in the grass.

Reaching into the pocket of Grace's shorts, Ellie hands me her puffer. Putting it into her mouth, I press the top like Mama showed me, making a loud sound comes out of the tube. Grace doesn't respond.

"Grace, breathe it in. Please," I beg. She's as blue as her plaid shorts. "Go get Mama, Ellie. Now!" My body shakes. Pressing the button again and again, Grace's body goes limp.

Mama rushes to my side, grabbing the puffer. "Real slow, sweetie. Breathe it in. That's it. Now you got it."

Slowly, Grace takes in the air, and color returns to her face. I exhale, realizing for the first time that I've been holding my breath. Ellie helps Mama carry Grace to the truck. Jesse's down on his knees in the driveway.

Still shaking, I kneel next to Jesse, whispering in his ear. "What are you prayin' for?"

"I'm thankin' God for savin' Grace's life. We always gotta thank him, Lil, 'cause you never know when your time is comin'."

I sure hope my time isn't coming any time soon. Today is enough to scare me into praying. Saying a prayer right then and there, I pray for my sisters and brothers. I even pray for Jimmy, which is saying something, considering Jimmy and I don't see eye to eye very often. The truth is, I really didn't want it to be his time either.

"Grace has pneumonia," Mama announces after returning from Dr. Hardy's office. "She's going to be just fine."

"What if she doesn't get better?" George asks, barely above a whisper.

"She will, George," Mama assures him. "Don't you worry."

Before we leave for the market, I check in on Grace. She looks so peaceful.

"Hey," she says, her voice scratchy.

"Hey yourself. Didn't mean to wake you."

"I wasn't asleep. You leavin'?"

"Yeah. We're gonna miss you being there with us."

"Me too," she says quietly. She turns to Ellie standing in the doorway. "How are my pullets?"

"They're fine. I'll take care of them," Ellie answers.

"I feel sad not being with them."

"They're fine," Ellie repeats. "What's the speckled one's name again?"

"Dots. Don't forget. Dots is real special, and she deserves a special home."

"Okay, I'll see to it. You rest, and I'll let you know when we get back how many I sold." Ellie gives her a gentle hug.

Pulling out of the driveway, Ellie stares out the window of the truck.

"You alright?" I ask. "You're awfully quiet."

"I was thinking, maybe we should put off our birthday party, since Grace is sick and all. I don't want to leave her all by herself."

It never once crossed my mind to cancel my birthday party for my sick sister.

"Don't be silly, Ellie." Mama must've read my thoughts. "Grace will be fine. This is your birthday, and I won't have you missing it."

"Okay. If you're sure," Ellie says.

"Of course I'm sure. Why don't you tell me again what you want for your birthday?" Mama already knows what we want.

"I'd like a necklace," Ellie answers. "I saw one in Sawyer's with a shiny, gold chain and a ruby charm hanging from it. The one in Sawyer's is probably too expensive, so maybe you could find somethin' like it."

"I'll see what I can do." Mama smiles. "And what about you, Lillie Mae? What do you want?"

"She needs a dress so she can look pretty for Wyatt," Ellie interrupts.

My head shoots up, and I shove Ellie into the door. "Stop."

"Oh?" Mama's eyes go wide.

"Ignore her, Mama," I say, poking Ellie in the ribs.

"Ouch!" she shrieks. "I was just speakin' my mind. You know you still think he's cute, and you don't have a single good dress. If you decide to ever talk to him again, that is."

Ellie knows she has Mama's attention, and it's killing me. I've never shown a single shred of interest in a boy before now. Dressing up has been a burden that I've had to bear on Sunday mornings.

If liking a boy means I have to get fancied up and worry about what I look like, the way Ellie does, well I'm not interested. Besides, I don't even want to *like* Wyatt. I'm still brooding about the whole episode at church.

Aware that Mama is speaking to me, I turn. "What did you say, Mama?"

"I asked what you want for your birthday."

"Well..." What I really want is expensive and rather selfish considering our farm is about to be stolen out from under us. "I'd like to have a pair of Nike sneakers, navy blue with white markings on the side. I know they're expensive..." I pause. "All the kids are wearin' them nowadays."

"Hum." Mama starts to say something, probably correct my grammar. Instead, she surprises me. "We'll have to see, won't we? I've heard boys like girls in pretty sneakers."

She winks at Ellie as I slink down into the seat.

Chapter 22 🍊 The Rainbow

SUMMER thunderstorms are normal in Georgia, passing as quickly as they come. As the clouds roll in, the wind picks up, dropping the temperature a good ten degrees. Today's breeze at the market feels good on my hot shoulders. A sudden gust blows our tablecloth, nearly knocking the baskets of vegetables to the ground.

"Mama!" Ellie points to the sky as a flash of lightning strikes nearby.

"Time to go," Mama shouts above the wind. "Quickly now. Pack up the truck."

The sky opens up, sending a downpour. I'm soaked down to my panties. Mama shuts the tailgate, and the loud crash matches a clap of deafening thunder causing me to jump out of my seat.

As we drive to the square to wait out the storm, the rain pellets falling on the hood make click-clack noises. The lightning and thunder move on, and the sun tries to peek its way through the clouds.

"Mama, look. A rainbow!" Ellie points above the buildings where a full array of color spreads across the sky.

Mama gazes into the distance, her eyes moist. A small tear forms in the corner of her eye and spills onto her cheek. "My mama used to tell me that a rainbow is God's promise to watch over me." Mama hardly ever talks about her parents.

"I like hearing about Grandma," Ellie says. "What was she like?"

Mama sighs. "My mother was beautiful and kind. Everyone loved her. I still miss her."

"How come you never talk about her?" I ask.

"I don't know. Guess it makes me feel sad." We sit in silence listening to the rain as the rainbow fades in the distance. Mama clears her throat and opens her door. "Help me carry the baskets into Sawyer's, then y'all wait for me outside."

Steam rises off the asphalt, and the heat suffocates me. My damp hair frizzes in the humidity. I don't dare glance in the mirror.

Pulling two baskets out of the truck, I turn to Mama. "I was hopin' maybe we could look around a minute."

"Not today, Lillie. We need to get going."

"Yes, ma'am."

Slamming the tailgate, Ellie and I carry everything inside. After saying a quick hello to Mr. Rumsfeld, we saunter back into the sweltering heat. I'm hot and sweaty and want to go home. *What is taking Mama so long?* When she comes back outside, a gigantic smile fills her face.

"What's with the big smile," Ellie asks.

"I had a really good day."

Arriving home, Daddy and my brothers work hard on the new chicken houses we're calling E house and F house. F house looks like it is almost finished. Although E house is coming along, it still doesn't have a roof.

"Hey, Lloyd." I wave. Lloyd Eades, from Silo Farms, stands next to Daddy.

"Hey there. Heard y'all will be up and running in 'bout a week or so."

"Yeah?"

Daddy comes around the corner of the building. "Sure thing. Finishin' the ventilation, then the roof goes on."

"That's real good news, Tommy Ray." Lloyd answers. "Give me a call when you're ready. I'll send out the inspector." He looks at his feet, shuffling in the dirt. "It'll be good when you get some more houses."

"Hope so. Too many farms goin' out of business. I'm tryin' to make it work."

I get a sinking feeling in my stomach.

SATURDAY morning, my family crowds in the truck, Mama and Daddy up front and us kids in the back. Riding in the back of the Chevy to The Mill, the wind catches my ponytail and whips it around until strands pull loose and smack against my face. My brothers chat about the fish they plan to catch. I am anxious to talk to Uncle Chicken about our land. Having my suspicions about Duke, I've formulated a plan. I need to be sure of a few details though, before making any accusations.

Once we arrive, my brothers hop out of the truck and head to the creek, fishing poles in hand. Heading straight for Uncle Chicken, he's surrounded by farmers, so I decide to wait and talk with him later in private. While waiting, I meander down the hill to the creek to find Mary Olivia.

Mary Olivia and Sarah stand next to Freddie. Sarah's face shines so bright, she looks like a string of Christmas lights. Mary Olivia charges toward me, making my feet lift off the ground. "Hey, Lillie."

"Goodness gracious. Don't knock me down, Mary Olivia." Nodding my head toward Freddie and Sarah, I whisper. "Looks like Sarah's havin' a good day."

Mary Olivia rolls her eyes. "She's crazy about him, although I have no idea why."

"Me either. He smells like Jimmy after a ball game." We burst out laughing.

Mary Olivia holds her hands behind her back. "Got ya a birthday present."

"Where is it?"

She throws her hands up. "It's not here. It's at home."

"Ah, come on. What it is?"

Mary Olivia wags her finger in front of my face. "Not till next week. Come on. Let's play in the creek." We dip our toes in the cold stream as the water flow over the rocks. "I can't stop laughin' about Violet throwin' a hissy fit at the lake. She squealed like a piglet." Mary Olivia throws her head back and laughs."

"I know. It was one of the funniest things I've ever seen. She was as mad as a wet cat." The cold water creates goose bumps up and down my arms. "I'll probably pay for that one."

"Nah." Mary Olivia shakes her head. "What's Violet gonna do? Pour chicken seed on you in revenge?"

My mind reels like Billy's fishing pole. "That's it, Mary Olivia."

"That's what?"

"That's the answer I've been trying to figure out. I gotta go," I say, darting up the hill.

"Go where?" Mary Olivia rushes to catch up with me. "Wait up, Lillie. You're not makin' sense."

When we arrive at the door to The Mill, I put out my hand. "Wait here."

"Why?"

"Because I need to talk to Uncle Chicken alone. About revenge."

Mary Olivia shakes her head. "You're crazy, you know it?"

"So I've been told." Stepping inside, I wait.

The parking lot nearly empty, Uncle Chicken places a bag of seed in the back of someone's truck before heading my way. He smiles through his toothless gums. "Well, if it ain't the old twin."

"I'm not old yet, Uncle Chicken," I retort.

He chuckles. "So, whatcha got fur me today?"

"Okay, ready? What is nine thousand, six hundred fifteen, times twelve thousand, three hundred eighteen?"

Before I can say all done, he spits out an answer. "One hundred eighteen million, four hundred thirty-seven thousand, five hundred and...wait, seventy."

"Amazing. How do you do that?" I ask, shaking my head in wonder.

"Ya gotta stay in school, Lillie Mae." He always says the same thing.

"I'll stay in school. Promise. Right now, though, I got a serious problem that needs your help."

"Whatcha got?"

Glancing around, the coast is clear. "What's our land worth? If Daddy were to sell it, I mean?"

He frowns and curls his lips over his gums. "Why ya askin'?"

Leaning in close, I whisper. "I have reason to believe that Duke Holt is tryin' to steal our land."

"That's some story. Where'd ya hear somethin' like that?"

"Pappy."

His eyes go wide. "Pappy?"

"Yep. He said Duke's been wantin' to get revenge on my Daddy ever since high school. You know about that?"

He pauses before answering. "Yep."

"I knew it. I knew if I asked an old person, I mean, someone like yourself, that I'd get to the truth. So, is it true?"

"Which part?"

Throwing both hands in the air, I let out an exaggerated grunt. "That Duke's tryin' to get revenge on my Daddy?"

"Don't know." Uncle Chicken rubs his chin.

"Well, I think he is. He says he has an investor, but I'm not convinced."

"So what do you want me to do?"

"Find out who Duke's mysterious buyer is. Please."

He tilts his head to one side. "Whatcha gonna do with the information once ya have it?"

"Don't know yet." Frowning, my lips curve downward. "I think I'll know when the time comes."

He cocks his head to the other side and scratches what's left of his hair. "Hum. Maybe ya should talk to yur daddy 'bout all this."

"No. I don't want him to know I've been doing some detective work." He starts to walk away. "Please, Uncle Chicken," I beg.

Turning back around, he rubs his chin again. "Well, I'll look into it, Lillie. But first, ya gotta promise me somethin'."

"O-kay."

"Promise me you'll stay out of trouble."

Not able to look him in the eye, my body shudders. "I promise I'll try. Please, see what you find out about Mr. Holt, before it's too late."

Chapter 24  My Birthday

ELLIE SPINS around our room, showing off her pink and white checkered shorts and white blouse. Grace motions to my matching outfit. "Y'all look so purty."

"It's pretty, not purty," Ellie corrects, tickling Grace.

Wanting to show off my outfit and hair, I skip down the hall. Daddy sits on the flowered couch in the family room watching the Atlanta Braves game, so I step in front of the TV. Daddy looks around me as if I'm not there.

Mama gasps. "Oh, Lillie Mae. You look beautiful."

Daddy glances away from the TV. "Hey there. Where'd ya get those curls?"

"Ellie fixed my hair. Isn't it pretty?"

"Yep. Mighty pretty," he answers, staring at the TV.

"Who's pretty?" Jesse asks, strolling in the front door. "Whoa, Lil. You clean up good."

"Thanks." I smile.

"Who's ready for presents?" Mama shouts.

"Presents," George yelps, bounding in the room.

"Ellie," I shriek. "Come on."

"Tommy Ray, turn the volume down," Mama orders. "It's birthday time."

Ellie and Grace bound into the family room and Jimmy and Billy sit on the couch with Daddy, staring at the TV.

"Three to one? What's wrong with Braves today?" Jimmy barks.

"Jimmy, hush now. Let the girls open their gifts," Mama scolds. She hands Ellie and me each a wrapped present.

"You go first, Ellie," I say. Ellie peels the paper, careful not to rip a single piece. "Oh for Pete's sake. Just open it."

Ellie peeks inside and lets out a loud shrill. She holds up a beautiful gold chain with a ruby red charm.

"It's perfect. I love it, Mama! Thank you." Ellie falls into Mama's arms. "Lillie, it's our birthstone."

"Let me fasten it for you, Ellie," Mama says.

Ellie stares at her necklace and rubs the charm between her fingers. "I'll never take it off. Ever. Lillie, open your present now."

I'm not near as careful as Ellie and rip the paper to shreds. A brown cardboard box, the right size for a pair of sneakers, sits on my lap. Peeking inside, I gasp.

"What is it?" Ellie squeals.

"Nike sneakers! Navy blue with white markings. Thank you, Mama."

Mama kisses me on the cheek. "Happy twelfth birthday, Lillie Mae."

"But....how did you afford all this?"

Mama winks at Daddy. "I have my ways."

Then, it hits me. Yesterday, when I was feeling sorry for myself because Mama was taking too long in Sawyer's, she came outside with a big grin on her face. Now, I know why.

She sold our produce and who knows what else to get enough money to buy a necklace for Ellie and sneakers for me.

Our family room may be small, but today it feels full of love. Seeing everyone happy for Ellie and me makes me smile. I guess that's how it is in a big family. Even though we bicker, deep down, we really do love each other.

Flying out the front door to Meemaw's, my cake should be ready by now. Wearing my new sneakers makes me run faster already. Hopping around the mud puddles from the rainstorm the other day, I leap up the back porch stairs as fast as lightning. When Pappy opens the door, his eyes go wide.

"My, my. Who do we have here?"

"It's me, Pappy," I giggle.

"Who's me?"

"Lillie Mae." He's teasing me.

"Didn't recognize ya with all them curls. Come on in and let's see if Meemaw knows who ya are. Meemaw," he shouts toward the kitchen. "We got us a stranger in our house."

"Oh gracious me, William, you leave that poor child alone. Get on in here Lillie Mae and let me have a look at ya."

Meemaw spreads frosting on my cake, so I grab her around the waist. She spins around, dropping the knife full of frosting.

"Gracious me." She turns around. "Well, look at you, Lillie Mae. Don't ya look lovely."

"Thank you. Ellie did my hair real nice."

"She sure did. I love it," she exclaims. "And look at them new shoes, would ya? Um, um. Them are some nice looking shoes."

"I know. Mama got me exactly what I wanted."

"Where's your sister?"

"At home. Probably fixin' her hair, or her face, or who knows what else."

Meemaw laughs. "That'll be you too one day."

I scrunch up my nose. "Tryin' to look beautiful all the time is too much trouble."

Meemaw shakes her head. "Wanna help me frost your cake?"

"Of course. Can I lick the knife afterward?"

"Yep. Grab a new knife out of the drawer. This one's a goner. Why don't you start on the chocolate side?"

The thick, white frosting spreads across the cake. When the knife gets dry, I dip it in a cup of hot water. "What do you think, Meemaw? Did I get it all?"

"It looks real good. Let's put the candles in and we'll be all set."

Placing twelve candles on my side and twelve on Ellie's, I lick the frosting off the knife and lick my fingers clean. I've been helping Meemaw frost birthday cakes for as long as I can remember, and licking the frosting is the best part. With a mouth full of white icing, I babble about my party.

"Mary Olivia and Sarah are coming. And Betsy. Me and Betsy became good friends last year in school. Violet kept picking on her, so I stood up to Violet. Me and Betsy's been friends ever since."

"Well, that's real nice of you, Lillie Mae. I'm proud of you," Meemaw says. "Why don't you run along now and lemme get supper started."

"Okay. See you soon," I say, bounding out the door.

As I head home, Jesse and Billy help me gather blankets and pillows for my slumber party. I suspect Billy is only helping so he can get to my cake. After dumping the bedding on Meemaw's family room floor, Billy heads to the kitchen.

"Oh no you don't," I holler, rounding the corner. "I worked hard frostin' that cake." Billy smirks and puts his finger inches from the cake frosting. I lunge at him. "Billy!"

"He's teasing you, Lil," Jesse smirks, grabbing me by the arm.

Pappy saunters into the kitchen. "Billy's tryin' to eat the frosting off my cake, Pappy. He's gonna mess it up."

"He is not, Lil," Jesse argues.

"Leave her be, Billy," Pappy says. "This is her special day. Boys, go on now. Lillie Mae, your friends will be here soon enough."

Following the boys outside, I flop down on Pappy's front porch. The humidity slaps me in the face, and my curls start to frizz. Ellie runs across the field as Sarah and Mary Olivia pull in the drive. Ellie and I race to greet them. When Betsy arrives, we tear open our gifts.

"Open mine first, Lillie Mae." Mary Olivia shoves a small box in my chest.

"Okay." I rip the wrapping paper and read the writing on the box. "Spy kit?"

Mary Olivia laughs. "It's perfect for you. It has everything you need to effectively spy on the grownups. Look here. It says, 'contains a microphone for recording'."

Ellie busts out laughing. "That *is* perfect."

"Um, thank you. I guess." A smirk covers my face.

As Meemaw lights the birthday candles, I shut my eyes and make a wish. Ellie and I blow out the candles, then Meemaw hands each of us our favorite flavor. Vanilla for Ellie and chocolate for me.

Stuffing my mouth with chocolate cake, I lick my lips clean of white icing. "What did you wish for, Ellie?"

"I can't tell you. Supposed to be a secret."

"Tell me anyway. Twins aren't supposed to have secrets."

"Well…" she says, smiling. "I wished for Duke and Daddy to get along. And I wished for a way to keep the farm."

It never occurred to me to wish for someone else on *my* birthday. "That's a beautiful wish," I whisper under my breath. And I meant it.

"You can wish for that too, I don't mind." She grins.

"Maybe one day, Ellie. Maybe one day."

IN SCHOOL last year, I read a book about a family who spent the summer vacationing at the beach. The book said the ocean waves make a sound when they crash against the shore. Mrs. Periwinkle told me that Georgia has a beautiful coastline with white sandy beaches and blue waters. I'd sure like to see that ocean one day. I've never been on a vacation. Come to think of it, I've never been outside the state of Georgia.

I don't know what made me think of that today. Maybe because summer is almost over, and fall harvest is right around the corner. Pretty soon we'll plant corn, cabbage, and collard greens. Meemaw cooks collard greens every year on New Year's Day. She says it brings good luck. After the summer I've had, I sure could use some of that good luck.

Mama chops at the dirt with a hoe. Setting it down, she bends over and wipes her forehead with the back of her glove. "What are you daydreaming about?"

"About the ocean. I'd like to go there one day."

"Me too."

"Have you ever been?"

Mama stares as if she is somewhere far away. "Once, when I was a little girl. My mama and daddy took me to Savannah."

"Where's that?"

"On the coast of Georgia. About five hours from here."

"That seems like a long way." I pause and pick up my gloves. "What's it like—the ocean, I mean?"

Mama smiles. "I can still remember the sound of the waves. A sound so nice it puts you to sleep. The sand between my toes was warm and soft. It's not like the sand we have at the lake. It's as white and soft as cotton."

"Do you ever wanna go back?"

"I'd love to. And I'd take you with me. We'd run through the water splashing in the waves."

"Can we go someday?"

"Maybe one day we'll all go as a family to the shore. We'll spend the night and go out to a restaurant..." Mama pauses for a moment. "Well, there's no use dreaming about what can't be. What we can do is enjoy this life we have right now."

The thought of never going to the beach makes me feel sad. "We could pretend this dirt is sand and the plants are waves."

Mama smiles. "That sounds fun."

We pretend to run through the sand. The waves crash into me, knocking me off my feet. Tumbling upside down, I swallow water. Mama rubs her eyes like the salt burns. We laugh and carry on for a long time. My screeching makes Ellie wander over from the other side of the garden.

"We're at the beach, Ellie," I giggle. "Watch out. A crab's crawling across your feet."

She squeals like a piglet. I'm having so much fun playing pretend, I almost forget I'm working.

By late afternoon, the sky turns dark as the sun disappears behind a thick cloud. "Look at the sky, Mama." This time I'm not pretending.

"Good gravy. The storm's moving in faster than I expected. We need to get home now!"

I throw my bag on my shoulder just as thunder roars across the garden. A bolt of lightning strikes near the woods.

"Hurry up, girls," Mama yells over her shoulder.

Another clap of thunder scares me. Covering my head with the bag, I spill the squash and pole beans. Ellie runs ahead of me and disappears, so I assume she and Mama must be home by now. Stopping to scoop the beans, I leave the squash behind.

A loud commotion across the yard makes me turn around and head back up the hill to the chicken houses. Billy squats on the tin roof of E house.

"Billy," I shout above the thunder. "What on earth are you doin' up there? It's lightning. Come down."

"Have to secure the roof first."

"It can wait. Get down."

Jimmy yells from somewhere behind the building. "In a minute, Lillie Mae. I need another nail. Billy's holdin' the roof on for me."

Daddy flies around the corner, arms waving. "You left him up there, Jimmy? Billy, get down here."

"But Jimmy said—"

"Now!" Daddy hollers. "It's blowin' up a storm." He turns to Jimmy. "Take Billy to the house, son. What were ya thinkin'?" Daddy doesn't wait for an answer. He rushes back to E house.

A sudden chill comes over me. The wind blows my hair in my face, and I scramble to tuck it behind my ears. A large branch flies across the yard barely missing me. I scream.

"Lillie, go home!" Daddy shouts from the side of the hen house.

"Where's Jesse?" I yell above the thunder.

Jimmy grabs Billy's hand. "He's at home, Lillie. Come on."

Stepping in a puddle, my new sneakers soak up the mud. When I reach the front door, a sudden gust of wind takes me by surprise, catching the door and slamming it against the wall of the porch. I pull with all my might to fight the wind and get the door closed, dragging mud across the kitchen floor.

"Good gravy, Lillie Mae. Where'd you go?" Mama shrieks.

"To the hen houses. Billy was still on the roof of E house."

"I'm here now," Billy shouts.

Mama points to my feet. "Your new sneakers. They're covered in mud. Take them off, and go get on some dry clothes. Y'all are dripping all over my floor."

I drip water all the way down the hall before stopping at the doorway to my bedroom.

Grace sits in bed reading a book. "Hi, Grace. Wanna hug?"

She crinkles her nose. "No way, Lillie Mae. You look like you just stepped out of the creek."

"Come here," I say, pretending to hug her.

"Stop it," she giggles.

Grabbing a towel from the bathroom, a shiny sparkle catches my eye. Ellie's necklace lies on the floor, the chain split in half. Ellie said she'd never take off her necklace. Walking back in my room, I drip more water on the floor. "Where's Ellie?"

Grace shrugs, not looking up from her book. "I thought she came in with you."

"No. She's not here?" I ask again.

"No. She went looking for you earlier."

Something doesn't feel right. The hair on the back of my neck stands up. "You mean she went outside?" I bolt to the front door, not waiting for an answer. The wind takes the door and slams it into the wall of the porch again.

"Close the door, Lillie Mae," Mama hollers from the kitchen. But I ignore her.

"Ellie," I shout. The sky is dark, and the rain makes it hard to see.

George sneaks up behind me. "Why are you so jumpy, Lillie? Afraid of storms?"

"George. Run to the back door and call for Ellie."

"Why?"

"Just do it," I bark.

"O-kay, o-kay." He sticks his tongue out at me.

I want to scream! No one is the least bit worried, but I am frantic. It's a twin thing that Ellie and I get whenever we have a bad feeling about each other. And right now, that feeling is pure panic.

"You okay, Lil?" Jesse stands behind me in the doorway.

"No. Something's wrong. Pray Jesse!"

My brother doesn't hesitate or ask a single question. He drops to his knees and prays with all his might.

A sudden gust of wind blows the tin roof off F house, smashing into the side of E house before flying across the yard. Lightning fills the sky as E house ignites into flames. Screams send shocks of terror through my veins.

It's Ellie.

"Ellie!" I cry. Bolting off the front porch, I sprint up the hill. Ellie comes flying out of E house covering her head with her hands. Daddy tears out of the building shouting something, his arms waving. The roar of thunder keeps me from being able to hear him. Grabbing Ellie's arm, we charge to the front porch as another bolt of lightning strikes nearby. Tears streaking down my cheeks, I hold up Ellie's broken necklace.

"You found it!" Ellie shakes her wet hair spraying me in the face. "I thought I lost it out there."

"I...I..." My mouth tries to form words, but nothing comes out. "I thought something happened to you, Ellie."

She tilts her head to the side. "I'm fine, Lillie. I went looking for my necklace. And for you. Where were you?"

"Where were you?" I shriek, holding her tight.

The flames from E house rise higher and my eyes flood with tears as an orange glow fill the stormy sky.

Chapter 26 🍋 Too Late

THE STORM subsides, leaving us cleaning up its disastrous effects. Exhausted, Ellie and I sit down in the mud while Mama and Daddy work nonstop. Billy's beat-up bicycle leaning against the side of our red barn catches my eye. Sprinting toward it, I throw my leg over the seat and pedal as fast as my short legs will go.

"Lillie. Stop. Where are you going?" I don't stop.

Riding on the path between our farm and Shortstop's, my tires hit a tree root, throwing me deep into the woods. Stunned, I sit up feeling dizzy. My leg oozes with blood. Determined to make it to The Mill, I force myself to climb back onto the bike. The wind blows my hair off my face, whistling like a tornado in my ear.

Coasting downhill, the scent from a nearby pig farm makes me gag. Deciding to take a shortcut, I race across a freshly cut field, holding my breath from the stench of the pigpen. My tires sink deep into the mud, forcing me to push the bike out of the field.

So much for a shortcut.

The Mill bustles with activity, so no one pays any attention to me. Setting the bike near the doorway, I don't bother to put down the kickstand.

Tired and out of breath, my hands rest on my knees as blood trickles down my leg. A worker carrying a hay bale nearly trips over the bike.

"Lord, have mercy. Didn't see ya there." Dropping the hay, he spots my leg. "What happened? You alright?"

Still huffing and puffing, I manage to squeeze a few words out of my mouth. "Where...is...Uncle Chicken?"

"Chicken? I think he's over yonder. By the straw. You sure you're alright?"

Forgetting my manners, I rush off without so much as a thank you. Uncle Chicken is buried deep in hay bales, barking orders to his forklift driver. "Over here. This way. There it is."

"Uncle Chicken," I shout. He doesn't answer. Stepping in front of the forklift, I hold my breath.

"What in the world?" the driver yells. The forklift halts.

Uncle Chicken's eyes go wide. He waves his hands like he's shooing flies off a cow. "Get outta the way, child."

My legs turn to stone, firmly planted on the concrete. "Uncle Chicken," I shout above the noise. "My family's in trouble. We need your help."

He whistles at the forklift driver and scrapes his hand across his throat. "What were ya thinkin'? Ya could've gotten hurt." He shakes his head and rubs his lips over his toothless gums. "Now, what'd ya say? Y'all need help?"

I nod.

"Follow me." Uncle Chicken shuffles away. He leads me to his office, complete with an old beat-up leather chair and a school desk. It sits in the back of the building facing the creek. He motions to the chair opposite the desk. "Now, why don't ya tell me what was so urgent that ya stepped in front of my driver?"

Salty tears fill my eyes. "The storm destroyed our farm today. You know the new hen houses, E house and F house that Daddy and my brothers built so we wouldn't go out of business?" I don't wait for him to answer. "They're destroyed. E house is as burnt as Mama's homemade bread. Nothin' left of it. I tried to put out the fire, I swear I did. We all tried. But it was no use." My head hangs to my chest, tears staining my shorts. "F house doesn't have a roof. I'm too late, Uncle Chicken. I couldn't save the farm."

He looks at me with a pained expression. Taking off his hat, he rubs his head. "I don't reckon that ever was *yur* job, Lillie Mae. Yur daddy wouldn't want you to think it was."

"But I wanted to help." Shuffling my feet across the bare floor, my cut leg hits the desk, making me wince. "It's all my fault you know."

"How do you figure?"

"Because. If I hadn't played detective and dug up the secret 'bout Daddy and Duke, this never would've happened." My body shakes with sobs.

Uncle Chicken stands up and walks around the desk. He puts one hand on my shoulder. "Now ya listen here. This ain't yur fault any more than my teeth fallin' out is yur fault. Ya didn't cause the storm, and ya sure didn't cause Duke to be a pig-headed fool." He lifts his hand off my shoulder and leans against the desk. "You were right, by the way, about Duke tryin' to get revenge."

My head shoots up like a rocket on its way to the moon. "I was?"

He nods. "Sure enough. There ain't no buyer. Duke's the buyer. Yur daddy's land is worth twice what Duke wants to pay."

"I knew it." Sniffling, I wipe my nose across the sleeve of my T-shirt. My detective skills had paid off after all.

"I suspect yur daddy knows it too." Uncle Chicken stares me straight in the eye.

My mind swirls trying to make sense of all the information. Hanging my head, I speak just above a whisper. "So, it's not my fault?"

"Course not. Yur daddy knew all along that Duke was really the buyer."

"Now it may be too late. We can't afford to rebuild." Pausing, tears start to fill my eyes again. "I don't wanna move, and I sure don't wanna leave my baseball field." Wiping my eyes with the back of my hand, I stare up at him. Then it hits me. "Wait." I jump up and the chair crashes to the floor. "We gotta stop Daddy before he sells, Uncle Chicken."

A smile spreads across my face as I formulate a plan.

Chapter 27 ✦ The Plan

LEAVING The Mill, I pedal along Highway Nine all the way to the square, car horns honking at me. Mary Olivia's farm is just beyond the next intersection.

Her front door ajar, I yell for her. Mary Olivia opens the screen door. "Lillie Mae? What's wrong? You look terrible."

"Thanks a lot."

She points to the bike. "Did you ride that rickety thing all the way here?"

"No. I rode it from The Mill to here."

"What? Why?"

"Can I just come in?" I bark. "I need some water."

Mary Olivia steps aside. Mrs. Montgomery stands near the stove taking homemade cookies out of the oven. "Lillie Mae. What a surprise!"

"Hey, Mrs. Montgomery. May I please have a glass of water?" Collapsing into a chair, I let out a loud groan. Sweat pours from my forehead.

"Sure." She sets a glass in front of me. "You okay, Lillie?"

"No, ma'am. Not really."

Mary Olivia gasps. "Your leg, Lillie Mae."

In all the chaos, I'd forgotten about my leg.

"Oh my, that's a nice cut you got there. Let me clean that up for ya." Mrs. Montgomery pats my shoulder.

"Thank you." Tears form in the corners of my eyes. Then, I spill the entire story. Every last bit, from the moment I played detective, until the storm destroyed our farm. I let out an exaggerated sigh. "That's the whole story. I have a plan that may keep me from having to move. But I really need your help."

Making a left turn into the woods, I pedal to the Johnson's farm, wanting to make it there before dark. There's no sign of Freddie or Tift. A loud crash from inside the red barn fills the deafening silence. Stepping off the bike, I guide it to the front of the barn, leaning it against the large wooden door. Pulling on the handle, the door opens making a creaking sound. Sunlight fills the dark room.

"Hello?" My voice crackles.

"Back here," echoes a reply.

A large John Deere tractor sits off to one side with tools spread all around. Underneath, a pair of muddy boots sticks out.

"Freddie?" A man slides out from under the tractor. *Gulp.* "Oh, Mr. Johnson." My insides jiggle.

"Hey there, Lillie Mae. Whatcha doing here?"

"Um." I take a deep breath. "My family needs your help, Mr. Johnson."

He drops the wrench onto the ground and stands up, wiping his oil-covered hands on dirty overalls. "That so?"

"Yes, sir."

He doesn't say anything for a second. He just stares, making me think maybe I shouldn't have come. "Your daddy know you're here?"

"No, sir. This is all my doin'. I'm tryin' to help."

"Uh huh."

"You see, I've messed things up real good. Ellie said if I kept stickin' my nose in the bee's nest that one day I was gonna get stung. Well, I reckon I have. And now, I'm tryin' to do the right thing."

Mr. Johnson listens as I share my plan with him. Hoping he will help, I hop back on the bicycle and rush home.

That night, I can't sleep. Climbing down the ladder of my bunk bed, I fall to my knees, doing what I should've done all along. I pray.

Whenever Jesse prays, he uses lots of big words, but I don't know which ones to use. Jesse's always told me to talk to God like he's my friend. I sure hope God doesn't mind.

"Dear God. I've made a mess of things. Again. I wanna be good like Ellie and believe in you like Jesse, but I just keep messin' up. Please forgive me. And please let my plan work. We need a miracle. Amen."

Chapter 28 🍋 Trying to Help

EARLY THE next morning, as the sun peeks its way out, it casts an eerie shadow on the lawn. Raindrops pour onto the grass. Rubbing my eyes, flashes of light reflect off the driveway. Thinking my eyes are playing tricks on me, I wipe them again. Loads of trucks stream down our drive.

Flying out of bed, I throw on a T-shirt and a pair of shorts and burst into my parent's bedroom. "Mama. Wake up."

"What is it, Lillie Mae? What's wrong?"

"There's some folks here."

"Who?" She sits up and rubs her eyes.

"You gotta come see." Mama follows me to the family room window. Her hair looks like a bird's nest on top of her head. I point to the yard.

"What on-" Then her face changes to a knowing smile. "Well, I'll be." Mama runs back to her bedroom. "Tommy Ray. You are not going to believe it. It's a miracle."

Mama and Daddy lock arms with me as I lead them outside. The rain lets up as we make our way up the hill to the chicken houses, my brothers and sisters following close behind. Banging echoes from the roof as one man nails a piece of shattered tin back on. Another holds a board, nailing it back in place. A forklift unloads pallets of lumber, dropping them next to the pile of burnt wood.

My mouth hangs open. I recognize some folks, but there are dozens I've never seen before.

Pastor Eddie rounds the corner, setting his hammer down. "The women from church brought y'all some breakfast," he says, motioning toward the barn. "Everyone brought their own tools to use..." He clears his throat. Pastor Eddie couldn't quite get his words out, which is kind of ironic considering he talks for a living. "Thought we'd help y'all rebuild."

Daddy's jaw drops to the ground. "Thank you. I...I don't know what to say."

It's hard to describe the feeling you get when you realize the entire town is here for you and your family. It's sort of like opening a gift you never expected.

Some of the folks are friends. Some are strangers. Some are even enemies.

Mr. Jackson and Wyatt stand in front of me. Suddenly conscious of the way I look, I cross my arms across my chest. I'm wearing the same dirty T-shirt from yesterday.

The rain gives way to a light mist causing my hair to frizz as high as our barn roof. Wyatt smiles at me without uttering a word.

Mr. Jackson takes off a pair of work gloves and rubs his chin. "Tommy Ray. I'm...well...I'm awful sorry about your farm." He gazes in the distance. "I was wrong about you.

Wrong about your family. My boy and I would like to help...if you'll let us."

He stretches out his hand to Daddy, who glances at it, then looks Mr. Jackson in the eye. Very slowly, they shake hands. Wyatt smiles at me again, and this time, I smile back.

Tears are funny. One minute you cry because you're sad. The next minute you cry because you're happy. I think Mama cries for both.

As we walk around thanking everyone for being here, my eyes play another trick on me. Coming down our long driveway, Duke Holt's red Ford gleams in the morning mist as mud flies in the air. Turning off the engine, Duke steps out of the muddy truck. Violet gets out on the other side and walks up the hill to the hen houses without so much as a hello.

Daddy stares. "Duke."

"Tommy Ray." He shuffles his black cowboy boots in the dirt and spits. I almost hear Wild West music playing in the background as he and Daddy have a showdown. Duke rests his hands on his hips making me wonder who is going to yank their gun from its holster first. "Heard the storm destroyed your farm."

"Yep. Bet ya didn't expect all this, though. Did ya?" He points to everyone helping rebuild the chicken houses. "It's over, Duke."

Duke runs his tongue across his teeth and spits on the ground again. "Yeah. I reckon it is." He opens his suit jacket

and pulls a stack of papers out of the pocket. Ripping them
in half, he drops them on the ground.

Daddy smiles.

"Reckon I owe you an apology, Tommy Ray." He looks
away. "Thought revenge would make me feel better, but all
it did was cause more destruction. So, I was wonderin'..."
He stops and looks Daddy in the eye. "Can you ever forgive
me, Tommy Ray? I know I don't deserve it and all. Still, I'd
like to have your forgiveness."

Mama squeezes Daddy's hand so tight, his knuckles
turn white. I stare at Daddy, expecting the vein to pop out
of his forehead. Only this time, it's not there.

Daddy sticks out his hand, and Duke takes it. "I've been
waitin' for this day for a long time, Duke." He turns to me
and winks.

Suddenly, I remember what Ellie said the night I found
out about Daddy's secret. "Anyone can change. That's what
forgiveness is for."

It just didn't seem possible for someone like Duke Holt,
who has spent his whole life plotting revenge. Then again, I
didn't take into account how God answers prayer. Even
prayers without big, fancy words.

Violet bounds down the hill, dirt smudged on her
shorts. In place of her usual fancy dress, she wears white
shorts and a white blouse. She holds her muddy hands in
front of her as if the dirt burns her skin, and she scowls at

me. "Hey, farm girl. How do you stand this smell?" She points toward the hen houses.

"I don't. I hate the smell. Darn chickens peck my legs every time I go near them. Hate them too." I point to the bruises on my bare legs. Her face curves into a slight smile.

"A little help here?" She holds out her dirty hands again.

"There's a water spigot over yonder." I nod toward our red barn, furrowing my eyebrows together.

Violet rolls her eyes and storms off toward the barn.

Ellie walks up behind me, linking her arm through mine. I turn to face her. "I thought you said everybody could be nice if they tried."

Ellie gazes at Violet and shrugs. "Not everyone can change overnight." She giggles.

"Yeah, guess not. Violet, she's—well—she's another story."

A familiar voice barking orders at everyone makes me look up. How Uncle Chicken managed to get himself up on that roof at his age is anyone's guess.

"Come down here, Uncle Chicken," I holler. "You don't need to be on a rooftop at your age."

His hammer dropping onto the tin roof makes a loud clatter. "I ain't old yet." He chuckles, showing his toothless gums.

Daddy helps Uncle Chicken climb down and pulls him into a *man hug*. At least that's what I call it when men shake hands and pat each other on the back at the same time.

Uncle Chicken smiles. "I've been savin' my money for years, hopin' to get me a wife. Seein' how that ain't gonna happen, I figured I'd put the money to good use."

Daddy laughs. "We can't thank you enough, Uncle Chicken."

He crinkles his nose and tilts his head sideways. "This ain't my doin', Tommy Ray. This here is Lillie Mae's doin'."

Daddy frowns. "Lillie?"

Throwing my hands in the air, I shove my shoulders to my neck. "What can I say? I told you I was tryin' to help."

Daddy bursts into laughter and hugs me tight. It seems strange that it takes a misfortune to make folks put down their disagreements and work together. But I suppose that doesn't matter now. What's important is that God provided a miracle. As the mist clears, the sun peeks out of the clouds, casting a rainbow across our farm.

I gasp. "Mama!" I point to the sky. "God's promise to watch over us."

Mama tears up. "It sure is, Lillie Mae. It sure is."

Ellie puts her arm around me, and the two of us stare at the rainbow. "Well, Lillie Mae. Looks like you're not such a Sour Lemon after all. Come on. Let's go get some Sweet Tea."

Acknowledgements

I am blessed to be surrounded by so many who have encouraged me in the writing process. To my amazing editor, Kimberly Coghlan, thank you for making Lillie Mae's voice come alive, and for all the extra help, above and beyond your job description. Thank you Sheri Williams, and all those in the Touchpoint Press family, for believing in The Sour Lemon Series!

To my very first reader, R. Lynn Barnett, who fell in love with *Sour Lemon and Sweet Tea* and encouraged me to get published. To Adell, for your endless stories of being one of four sets of twins, which inspired me to write the first chapter all those years ago. To Mendy, for sharing Uncle Chicken with me. To Danny Roper for teaching me all about raising chickens. To Country Folks Superstore, for keeping The Mill alive. Thank you to all of you from the bottom of my heart!

To my 209'ers critique group, made up of some of the best authors I know. Thank you Victoria Kimble, Jill Willis, Taylor Bennett, Burton C. Cole, Sharon Rene, Laurie Germaine, Kristen Johnson, Michelle McCorkle, and Gail Sattler, for dedicating countless hours to making this project become a reality and for pushing me to be a better writer. I'm proud to call you all my friends.

To my small group, Allison, Amanda, Debbie, Elizabeth, Hope, Sylvia, and Tamera, who have been with me through the ups and downs, and who patiently listened and encouraged me month after month. You are true friends.

To my parents, Gordon and Janet, and my sisters, Kim and Tara, thank you for modeling family values and extending forgiveness. You've been with me every step of the way and I'm blessed to have a wonderful, loving family. I love you! To my twins, Connor and Bryson, for the joy you bring me every day. I love you to the moon and back!

Most especially, thank you to my wonderful husband, Dusty, who believed in me from the very beginning and encouraged me to write. You are the real voice behind 2Wrds: Encouragement Inspiration. I am a better person because of you!

Thank you to the Lord Jesus Christ who has blessed me above and beyond what I could ever imagine!

—Julane